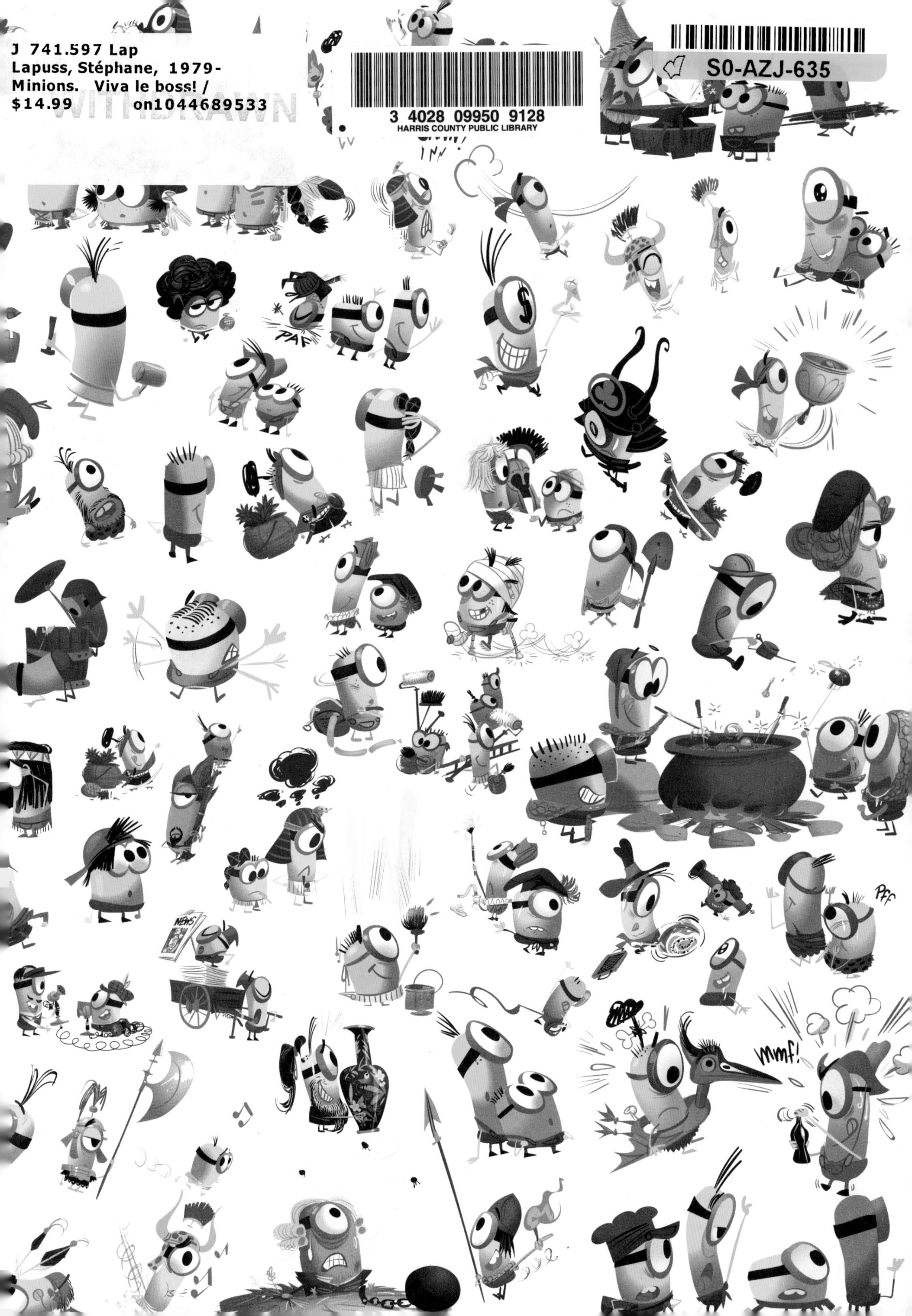
PAF
NEWS
Pff
Mmf!

MINIONS

VIVA LE BOSS!

TITAN
COMICS

Editor
DAVID MANLEY-LEACH

Senior Editor
MARTIN EDEN

Managing/Launch Editor
ANDREW JAMES

Designer
DAN BURA

Senior Production Controller
JACKIE FLOOK

Production Controller
PETER JAMES

Sales & Marketing Manager
STEVE TOTHILL

Press Officer
WILL O'MULLANE

Comics Brand Manager
CHRIS THOMPSON

Direct Sales & Marketing Manager
RICKY CLAYDON

Advertising Manager
MICHELLE FAIRLAMB

Head Of Rights
JENNY BOYCE

Publishing Manager
DARRYL TOTHILL

Publishing Director
CHRIS TEATHER

Operations Director
LEIGH BAULCH

Executive Director
VIVIAN CHEUNG

Publisher
NICK LANDAU

MINIONS: VIVA LE BOSS!
ISBN 9781787730168

MINIONS October 2018. Published by Titan Comics, a division of Titan Publishing Group, Ltd. Titan Comics is a registered trademark of Titan Publishing Group Ltd. 144 Southwark Street, London SE1 0UP.

Based on the characters from Universal Pictures and Illumination Entertainment's 2010 animated theatrical motion picture, "Despicable Me", the 2013 animated theatrical motion picture entitled "Despicable Me 2", and the 2015 animated theatrical motion picture entitled "Minions".

A CIP catalogue record for this title is available from the British library.

First Edition November 2018

Printed in China

10 9 8 7 6 5 4 3 2 1

BECOME A FAN ON FACEBOOK.COM/COMICSTITAN
FOLLOW US ON TWITTER@COMICSTITAN

www.titan-comics.com

TITAN® COMICS

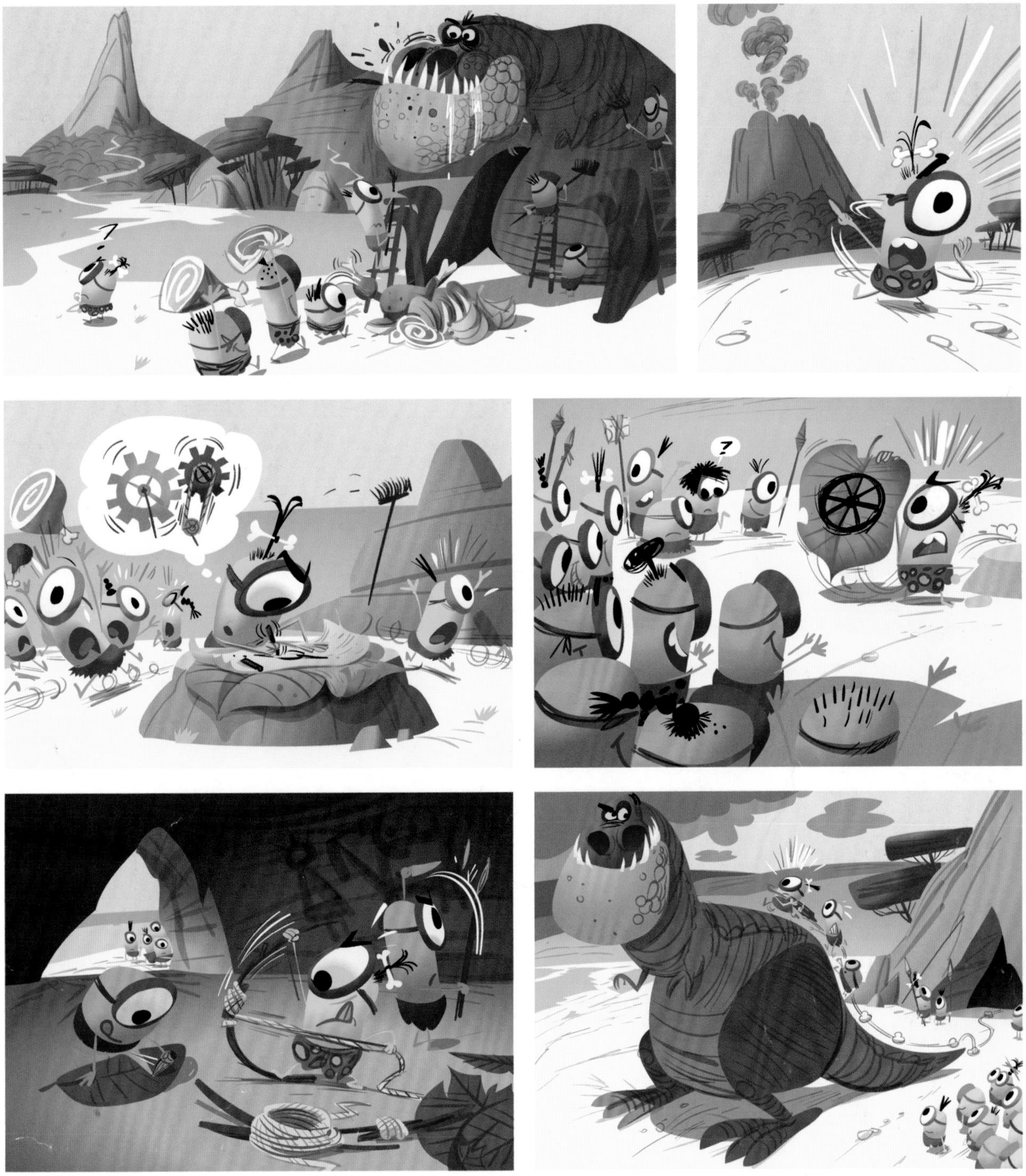

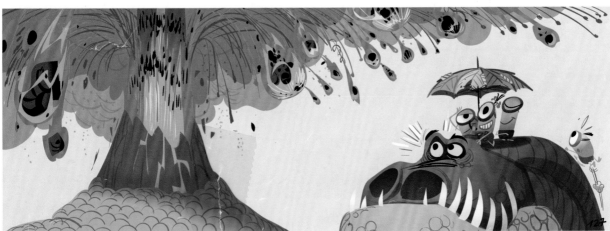

Renaud+Lapuss' 2018

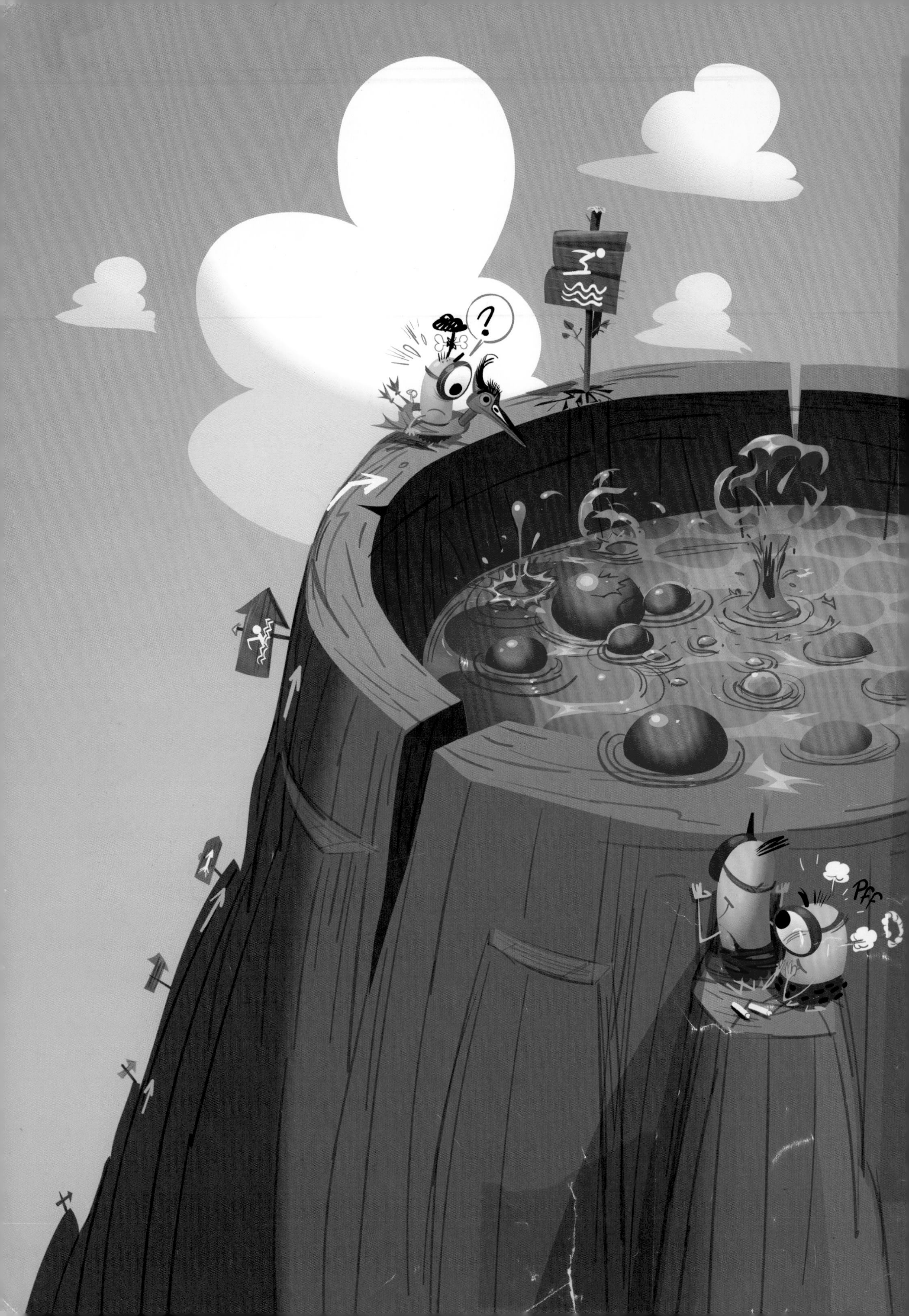
?
PFF

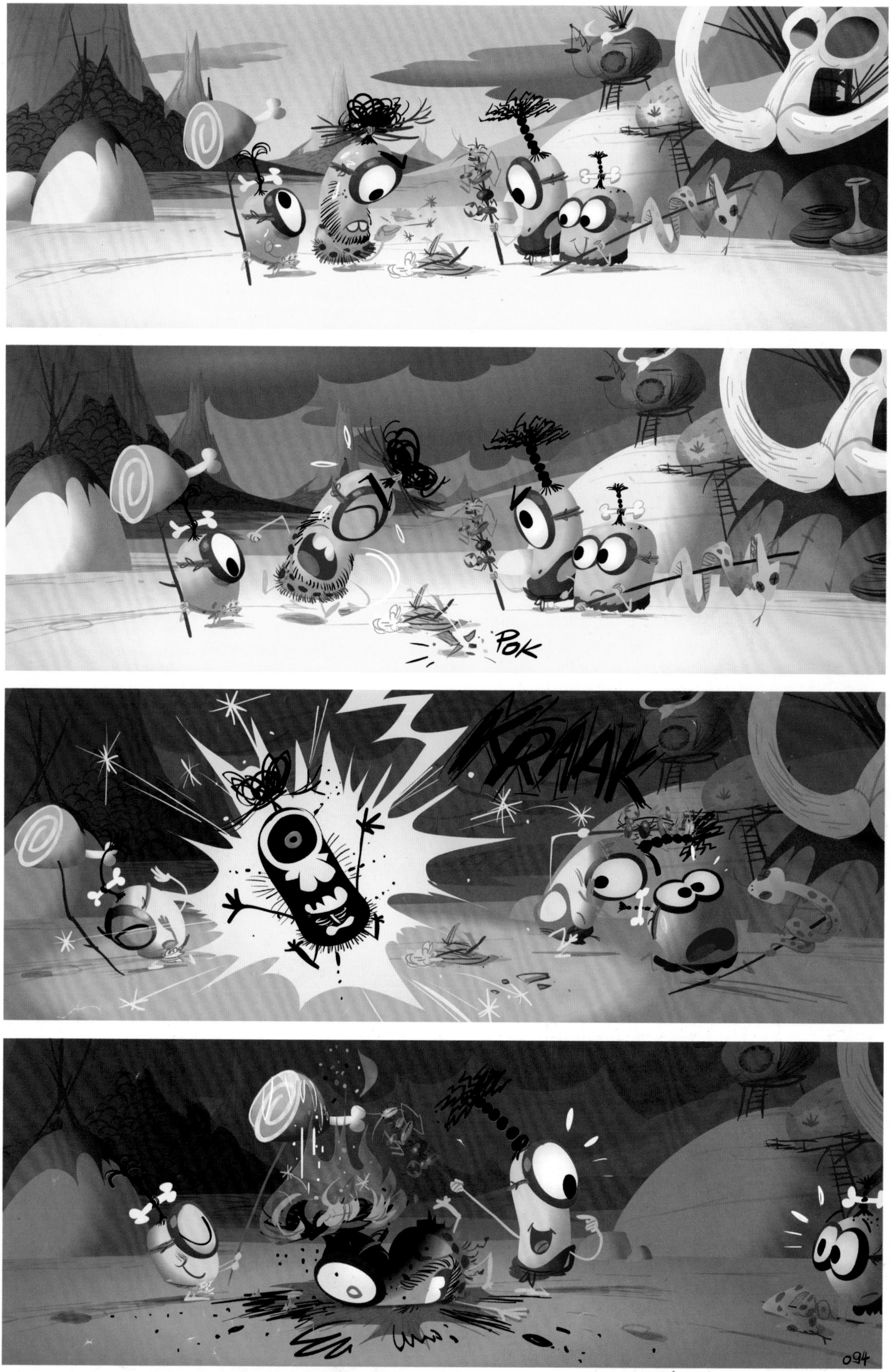
POK
KRAAK

Renaud+Lapuss' 2018

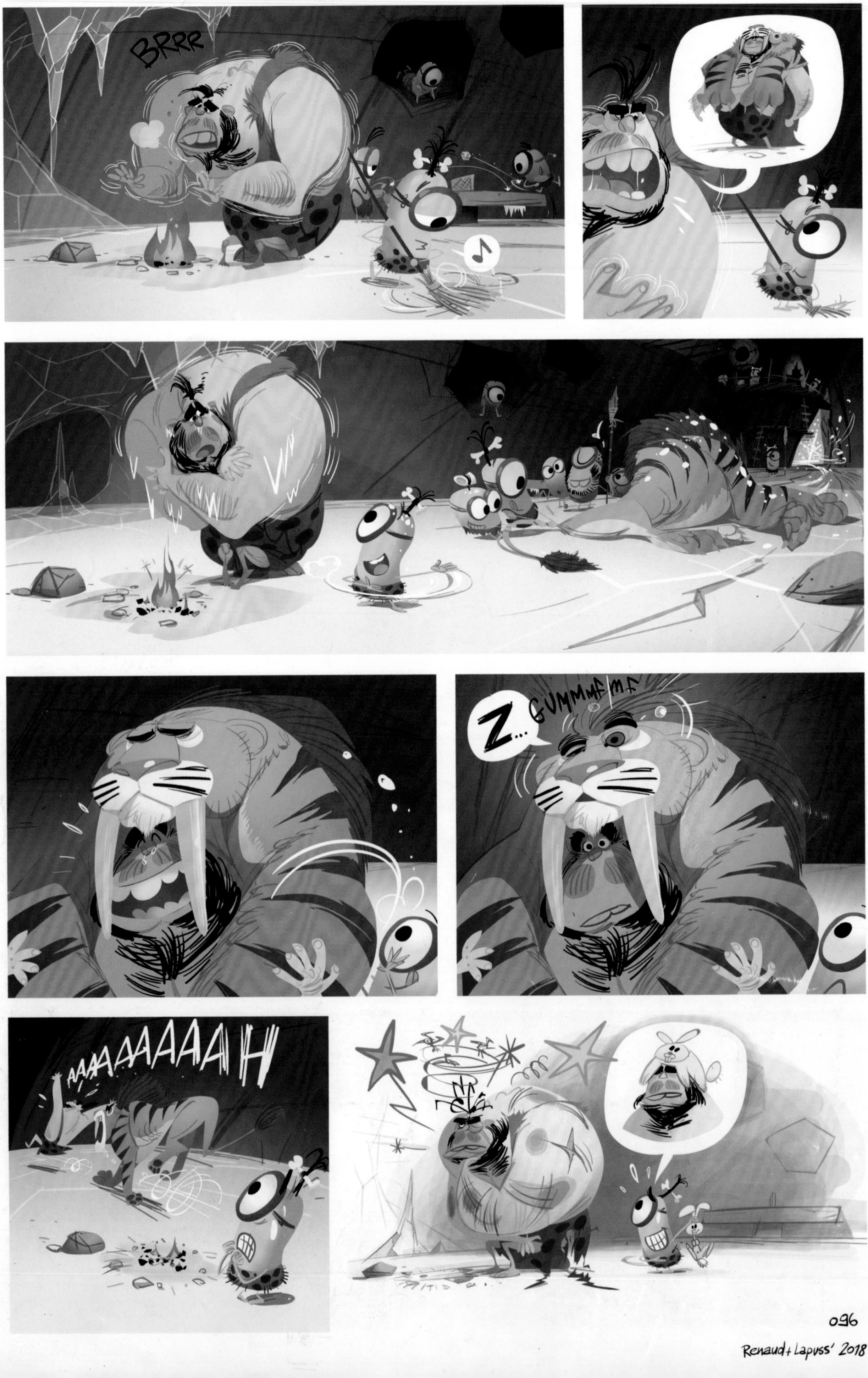
BRRR
Z...
GUMMMF MF
AAAAAAAAAAH

Renaud+Lapuss' 2018

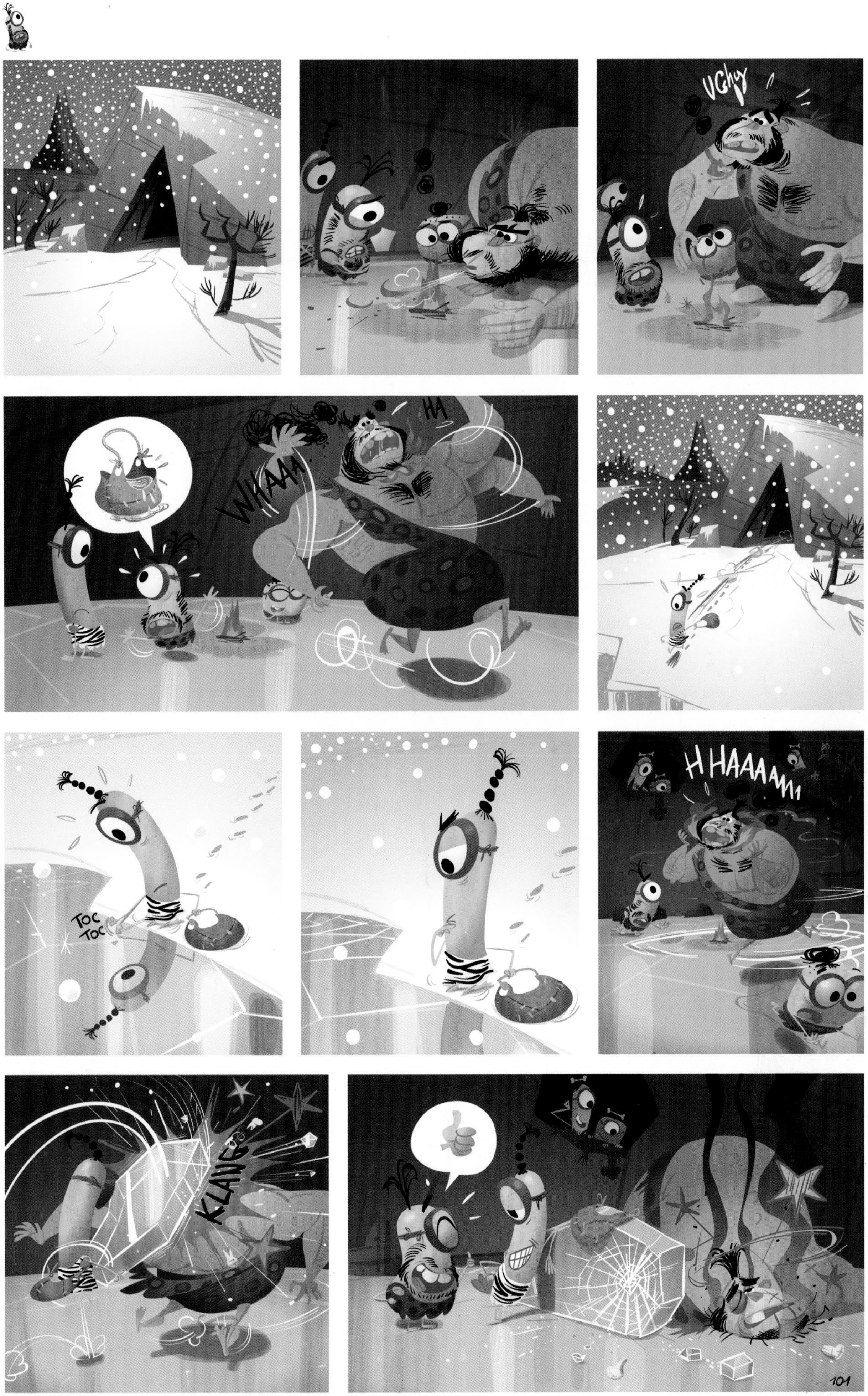
UGhy
WHAAA
HA
TOC TOC
H HAAAAAA!
KLANG

Renaud + Lapuss' 2018

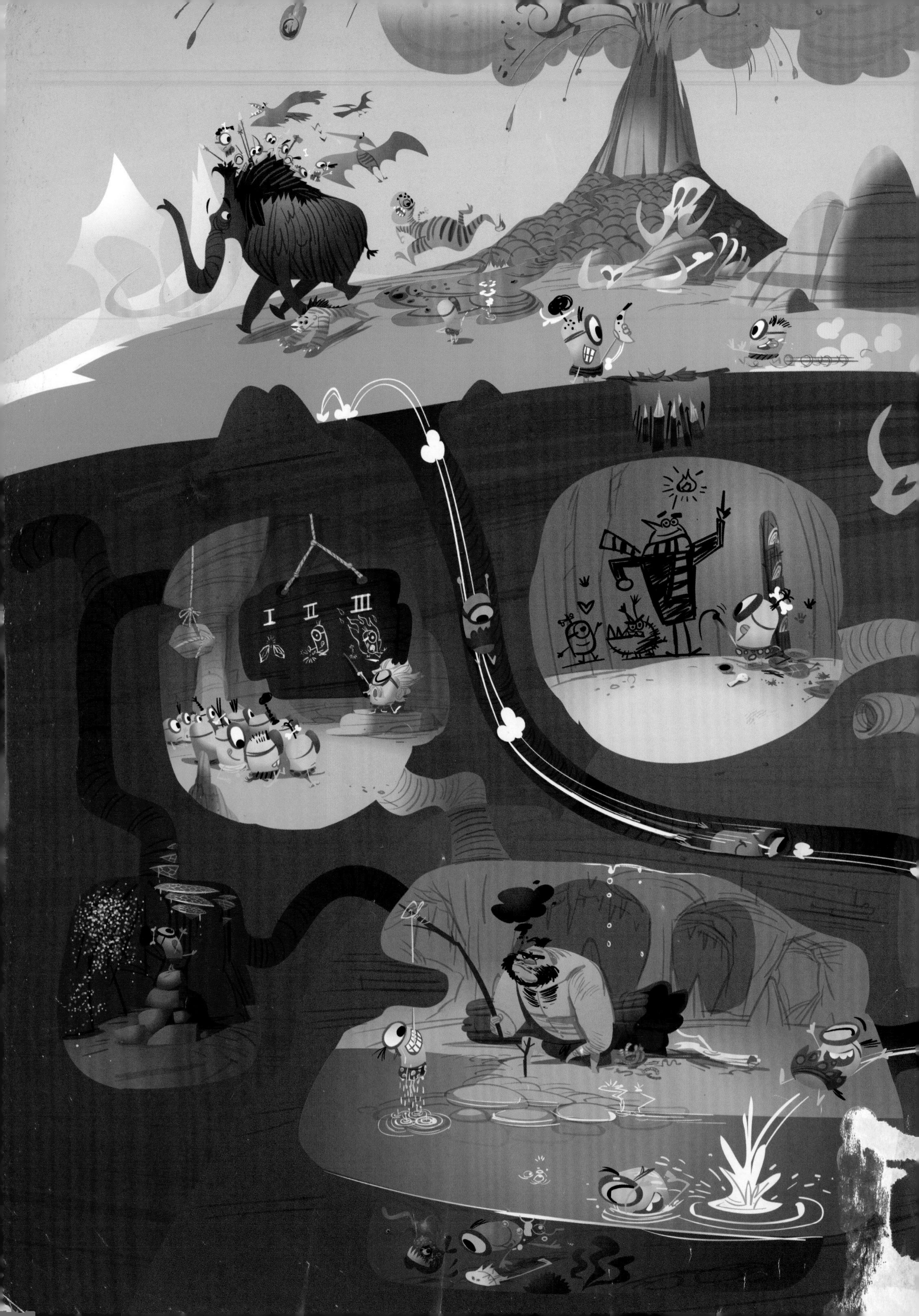
I II III

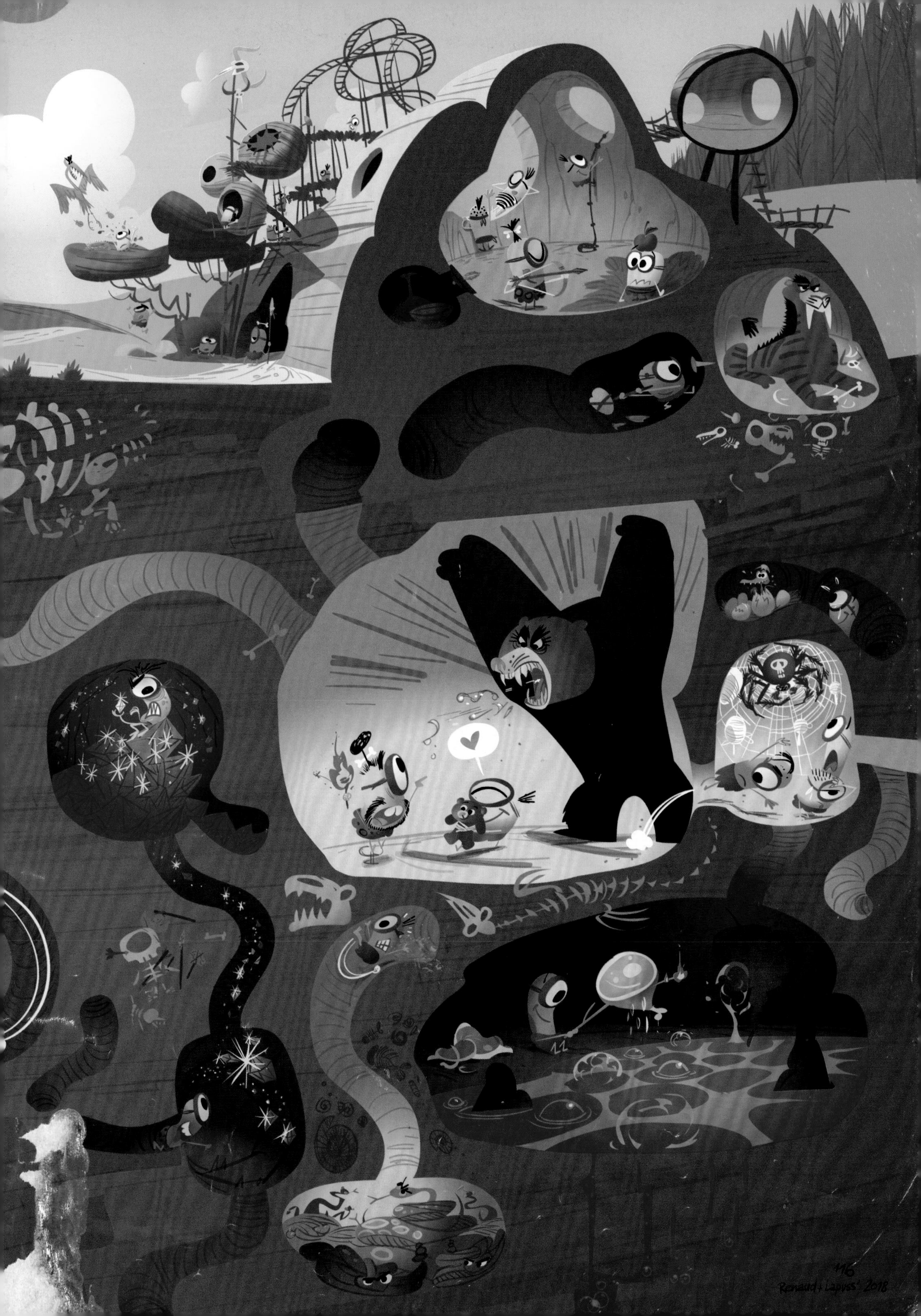
116
Renaud+Lapuss' 2018

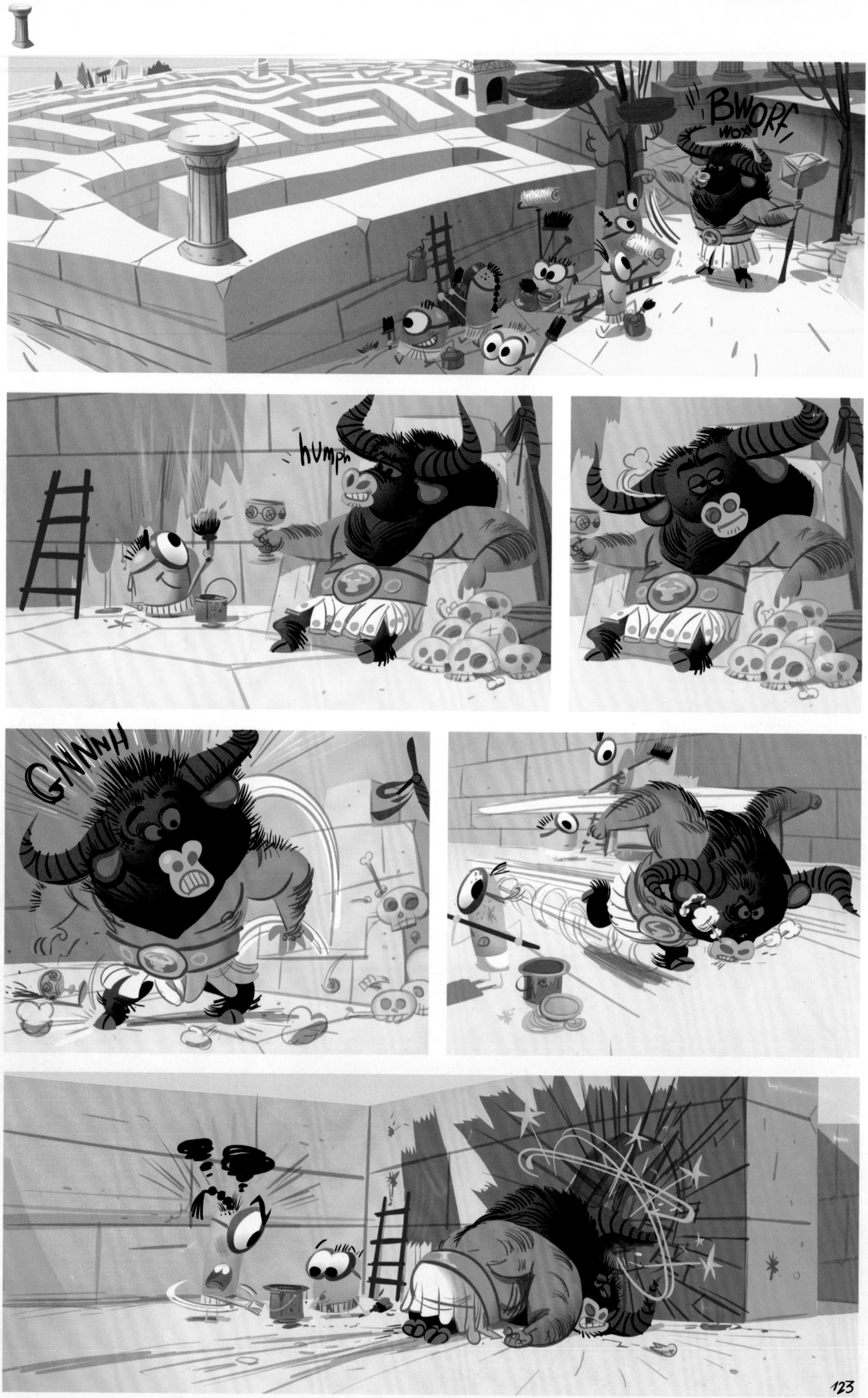
BWORF
WOA
hUmph
GNNNH

Renaud+Lapuss' 2018

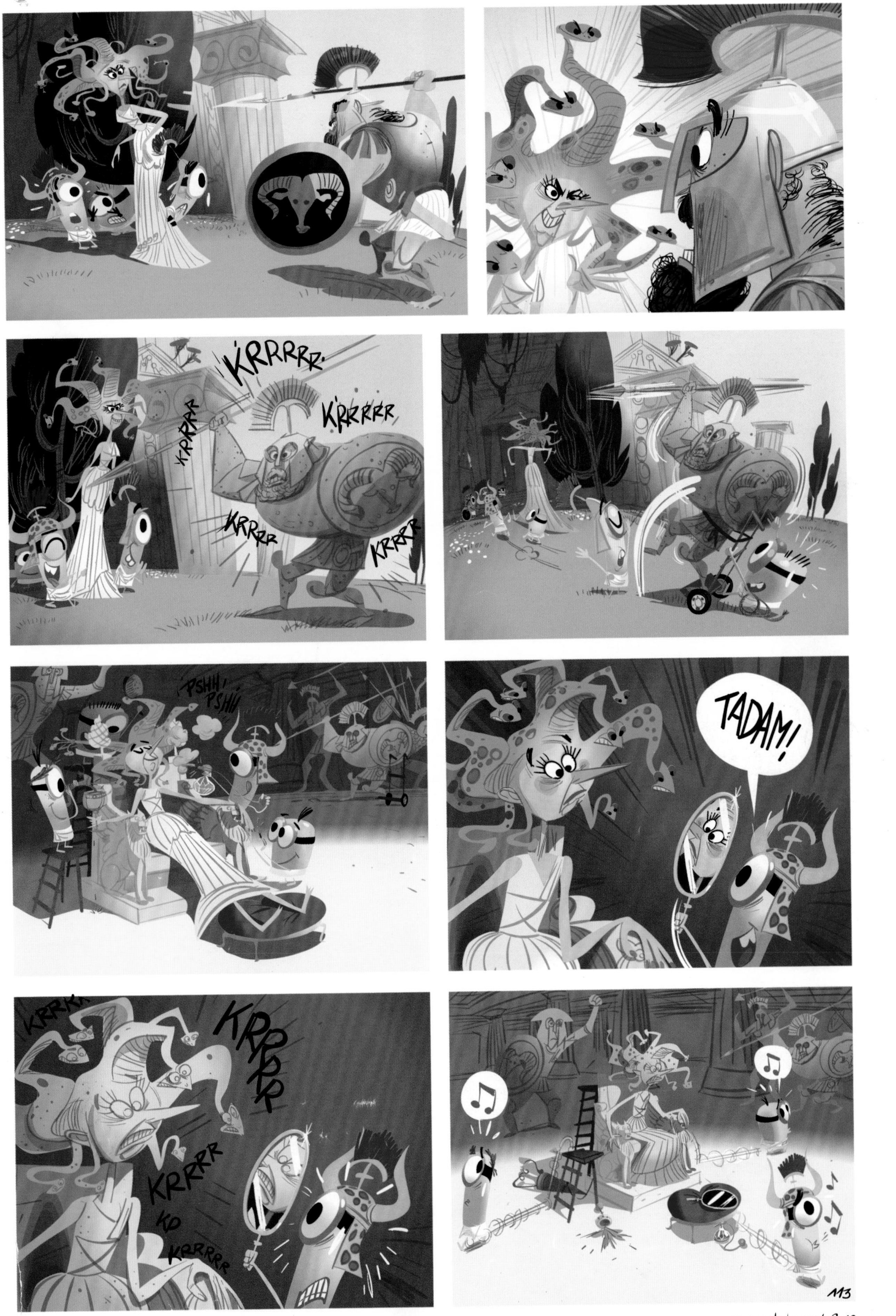
KRRRRR
KRRRRR
KRRRR
KRRRR
KRRRR
PSHH
PSHH
TADAM!
KRRKR
KRRRRR
KRRRR
KO
KRRRRR

Renaud + Lapuss' 2018

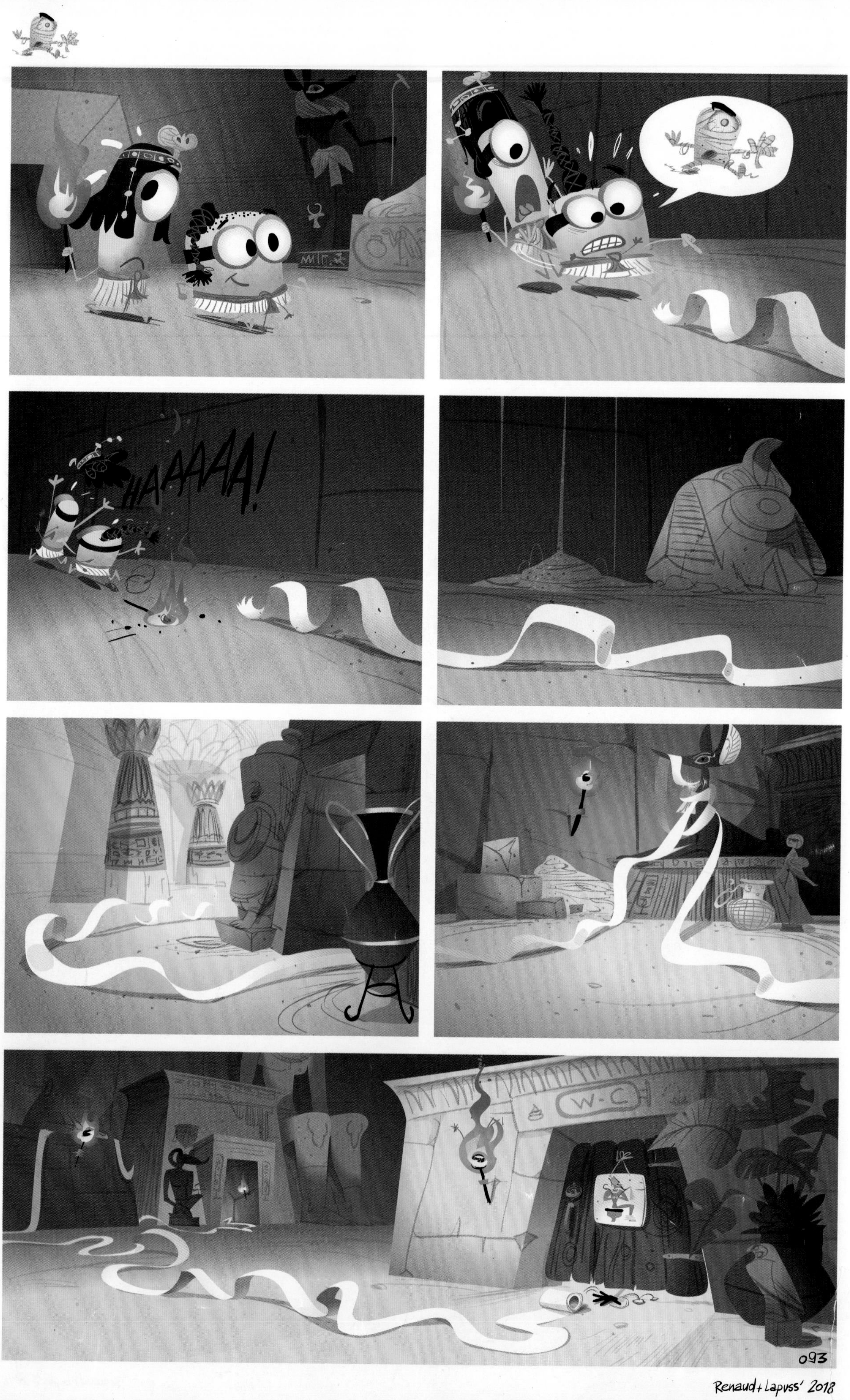
HAAAAA!
W-C

Renaud+Lapuss' 2018

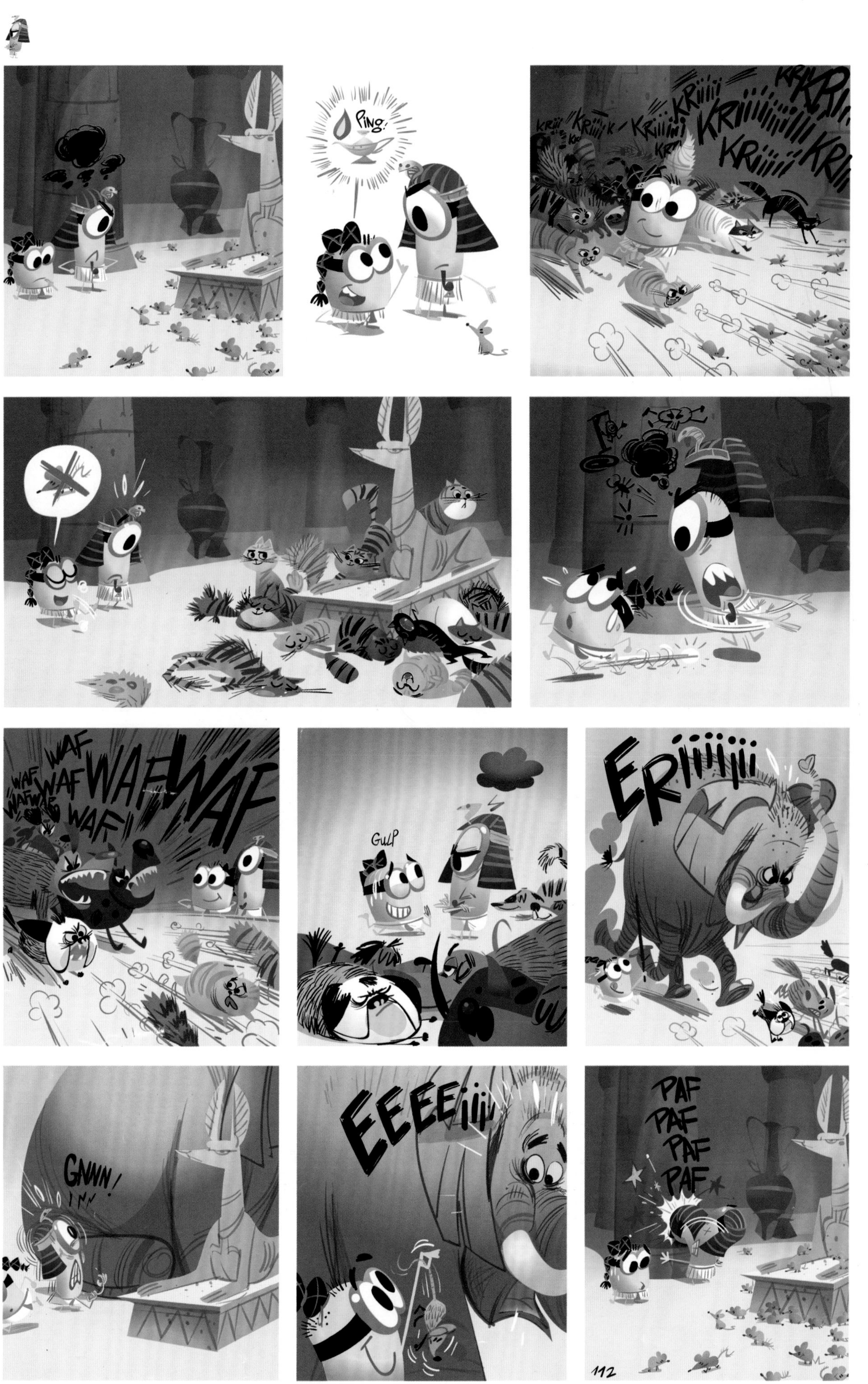
PING!
KRI KRiii KRiiii KRiiiii KR
WAF WAF WAF WAF WAF WAF
GULP
ERiiiiiii
GNNN!
EEEEiiii
PAF
PAF
PAF
PAF
112

Renaud + Lapuss' 2018

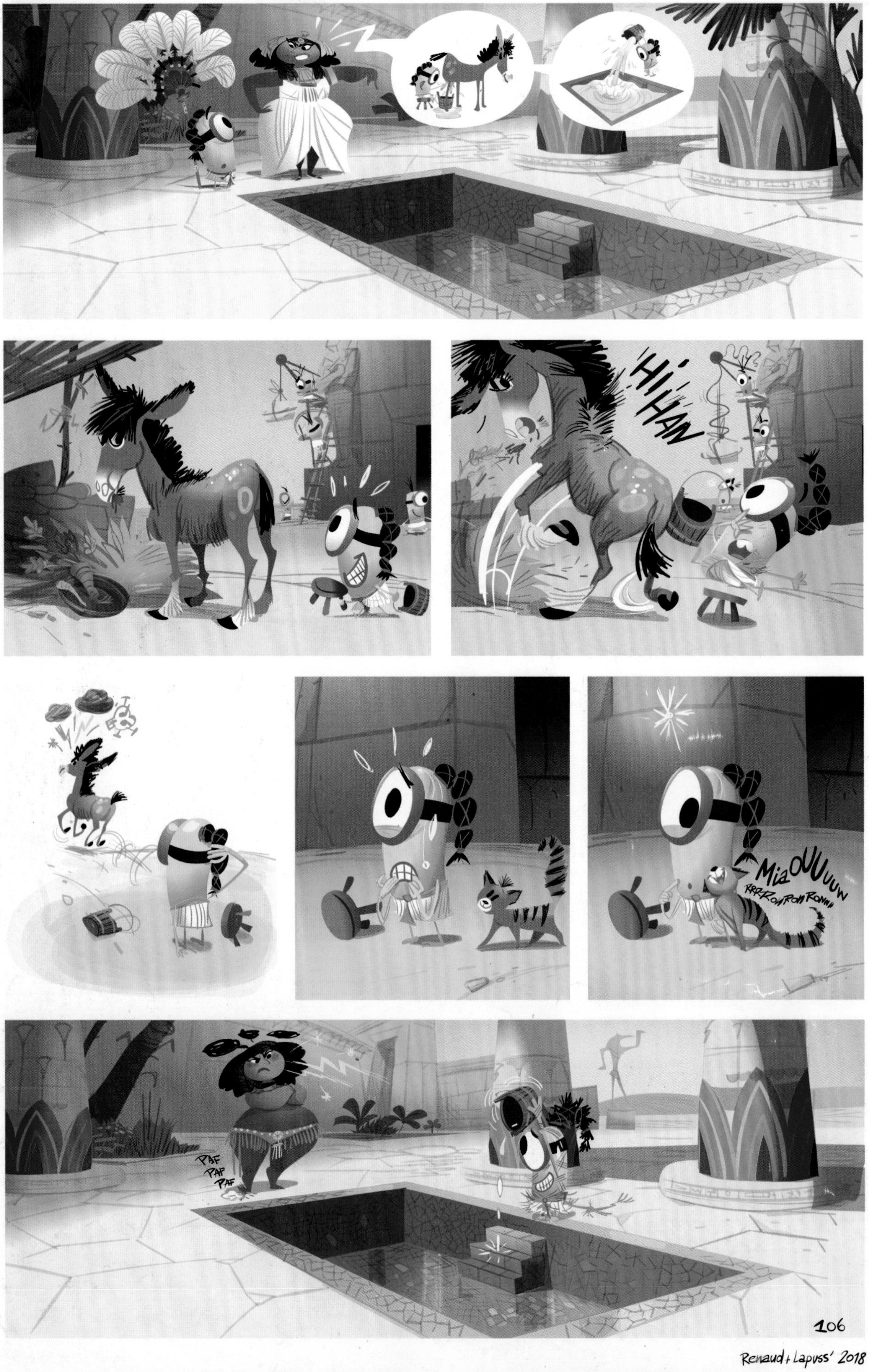
HI HAN
MiaOUUuuw
RRRRonRonRon
PAF
PAF
PAF

Renaud + Lapuss' 2018

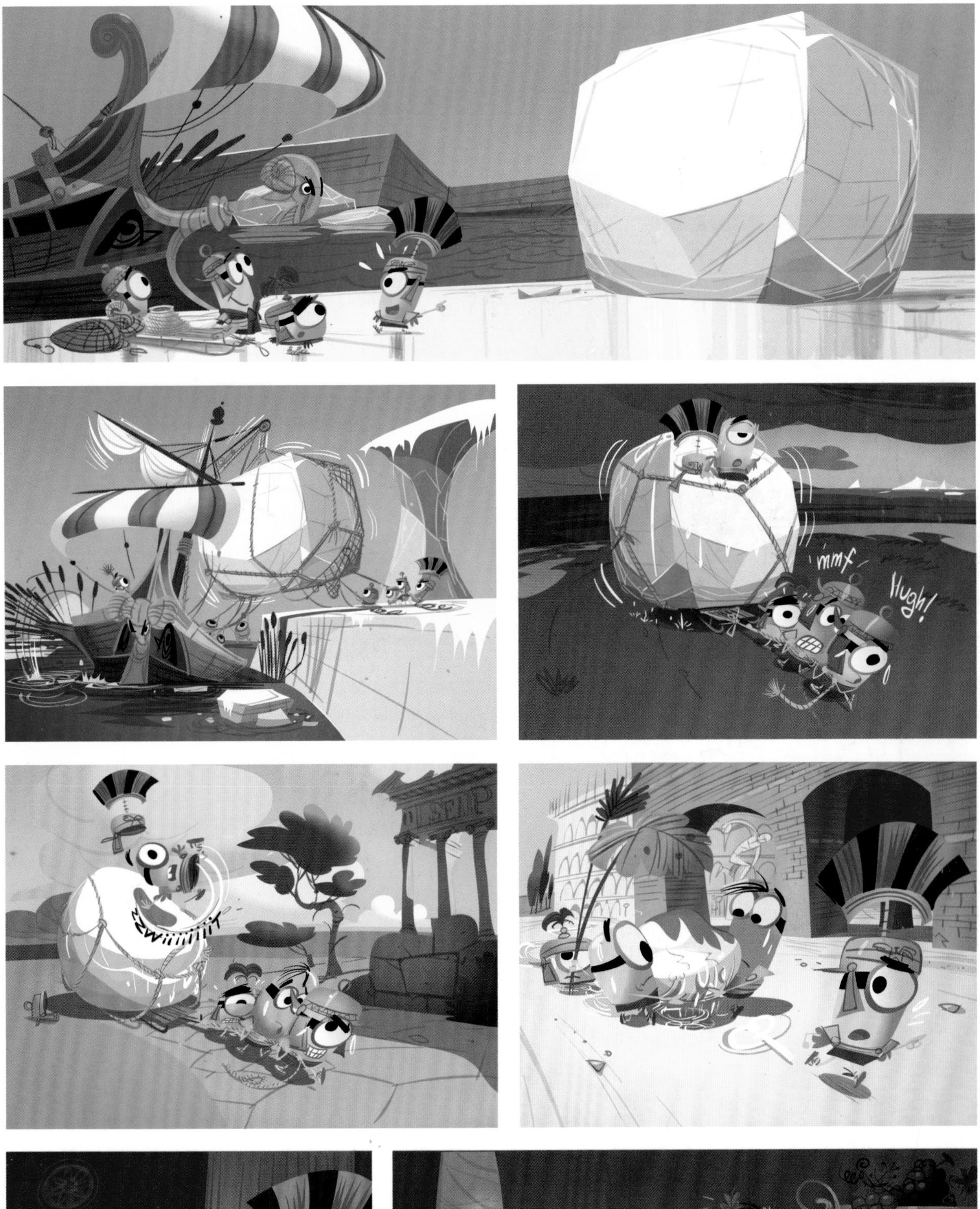
mmf
Hugh!
ZZWiiiiiiiiT

Renaud+Lapuss' 2018

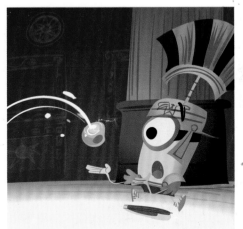

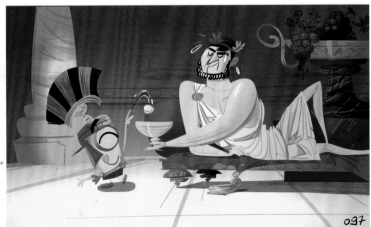

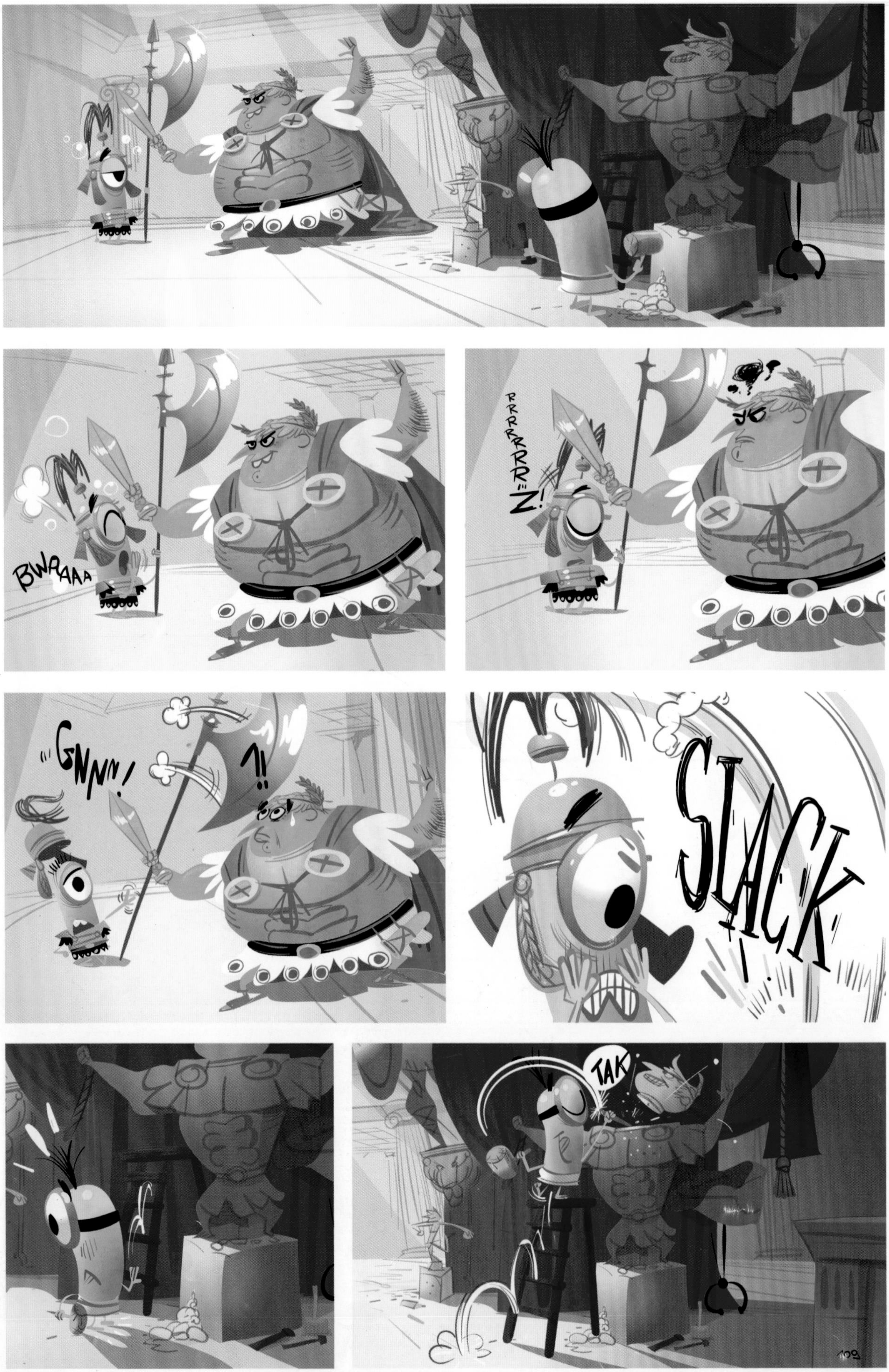
BWAAAA
GNNN!
SLACK
TAK

Renaud + Lapuss' 2018

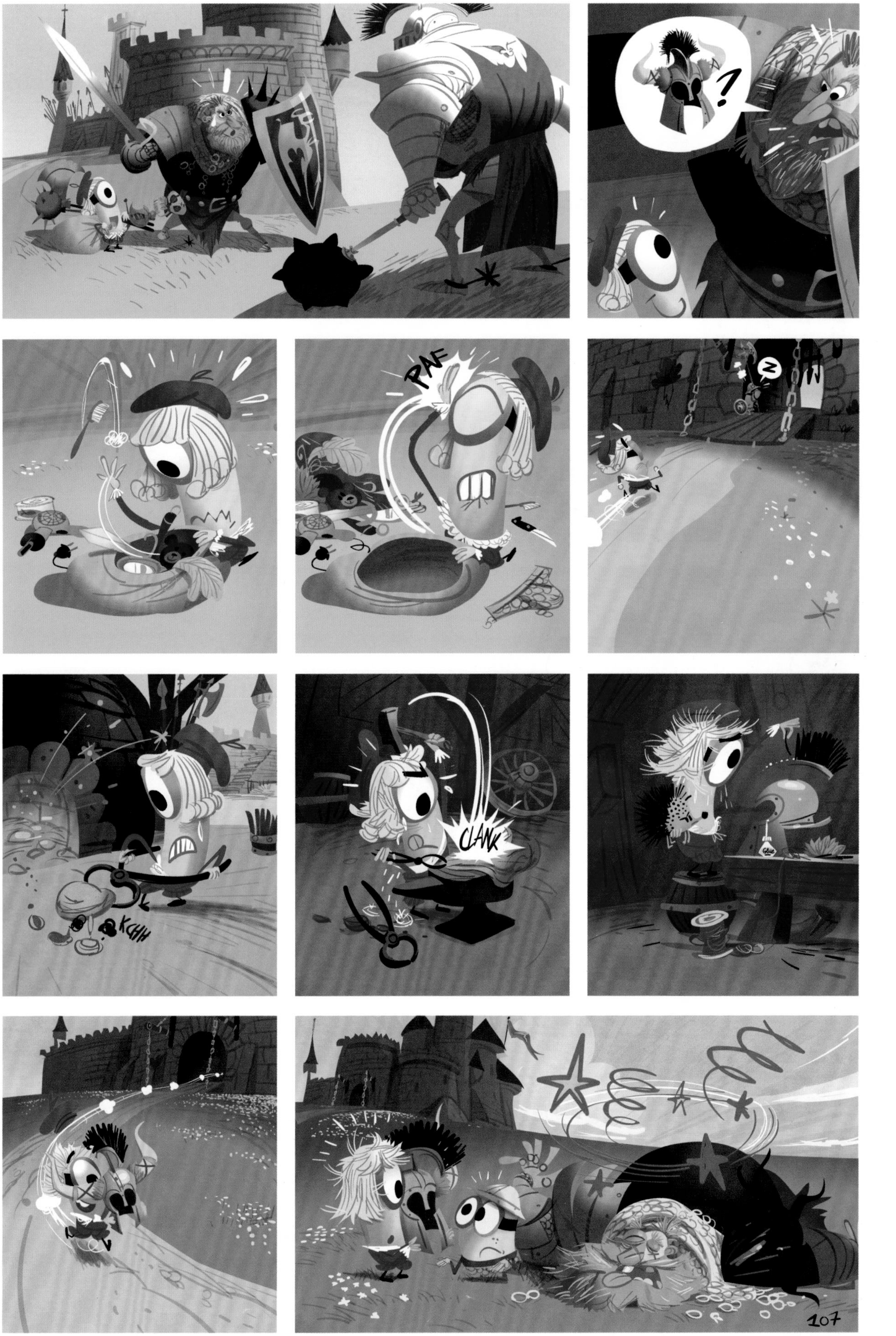
?
PAF
Z
KCHH
CLANK
Glue

Renaud + Lapuss' 2018

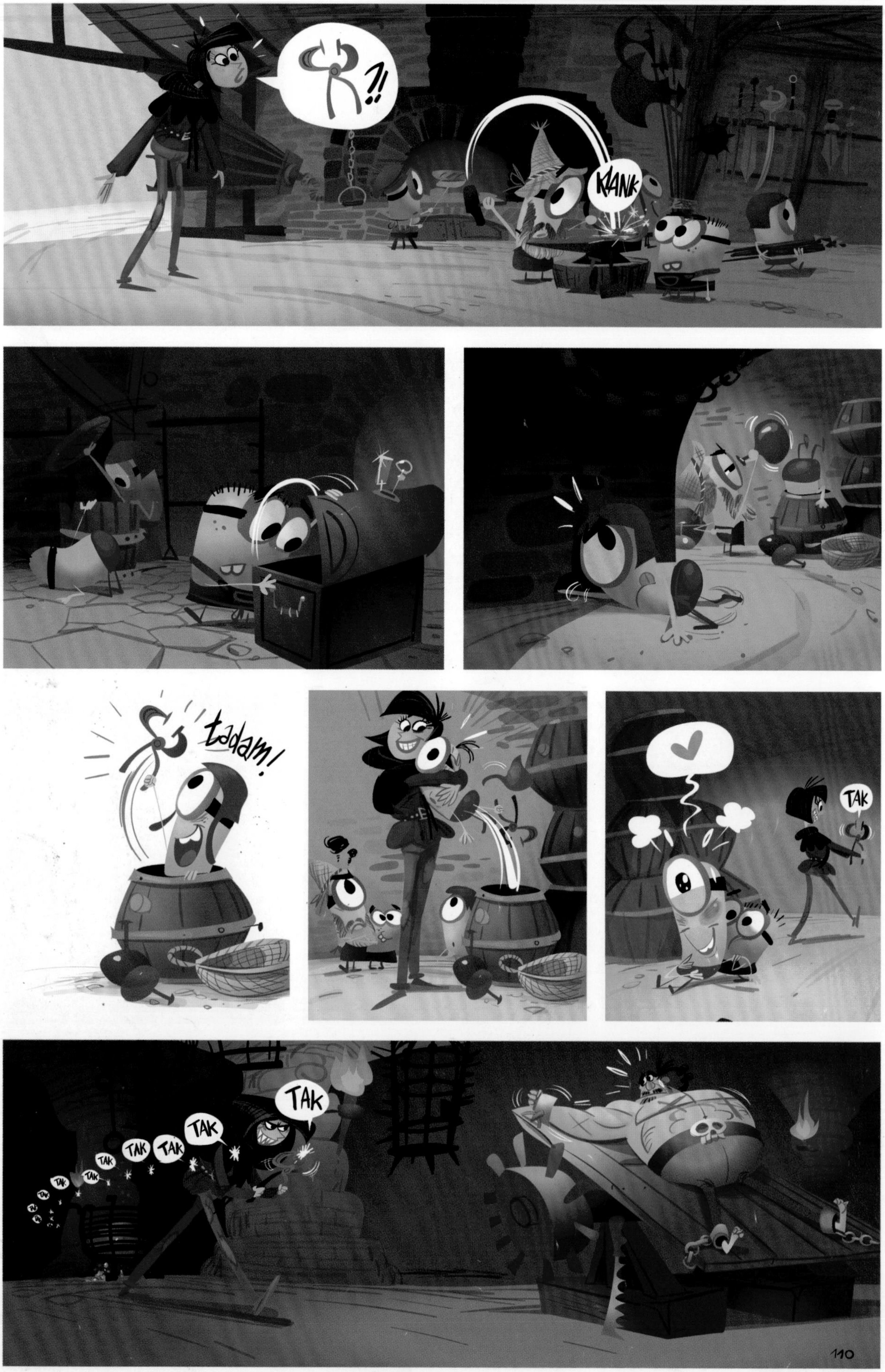
?!
KLANK
tadam!
TAK
TAK
TAK
TAK
TAK
TAK
TAK
TAK

Renaud+Lapuss' 2018

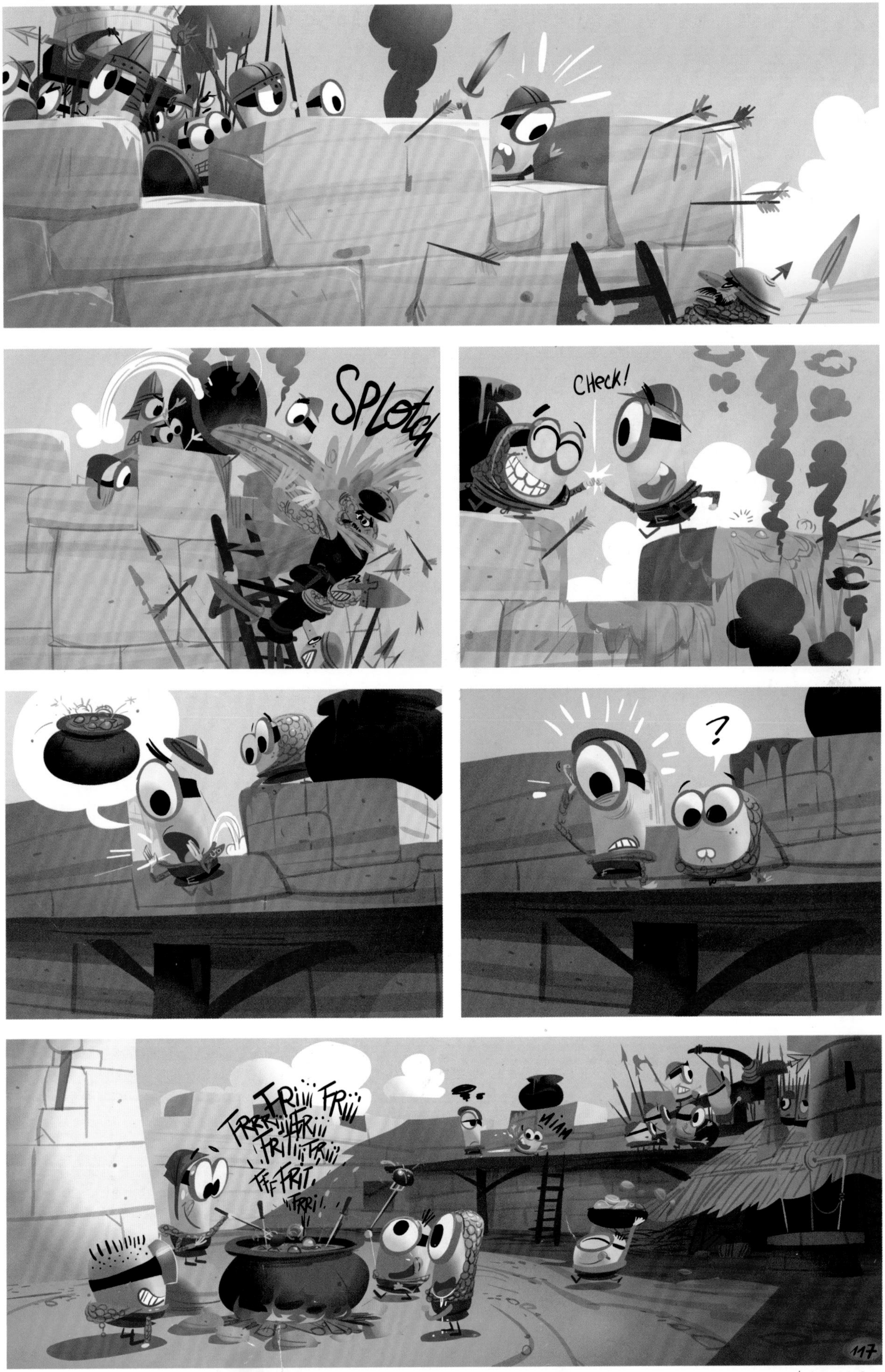
SPLOTCH
CHECK!
?
MIAM

Renaud+Lapuss' 2018

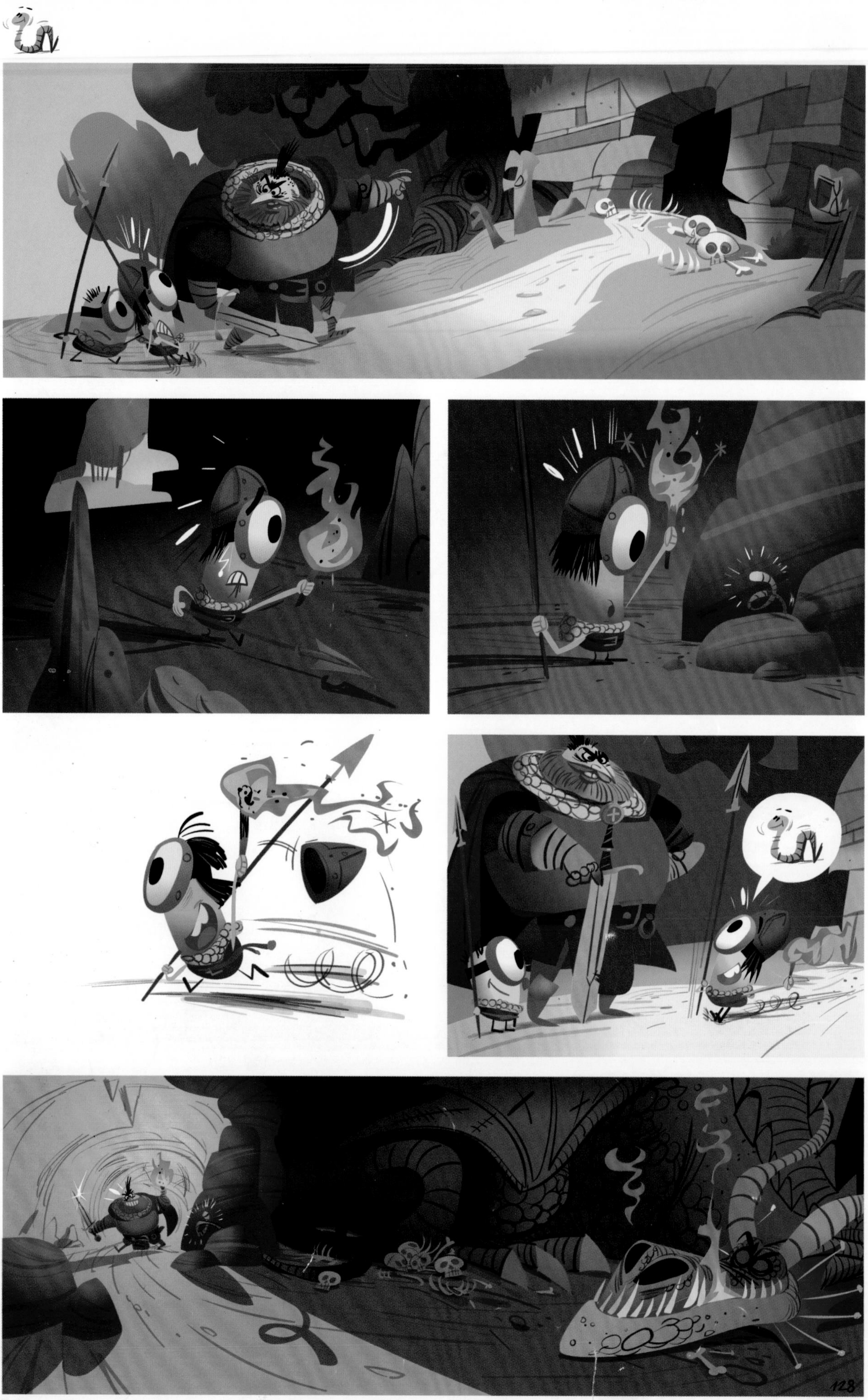

Renaud+Lapuss' 2018

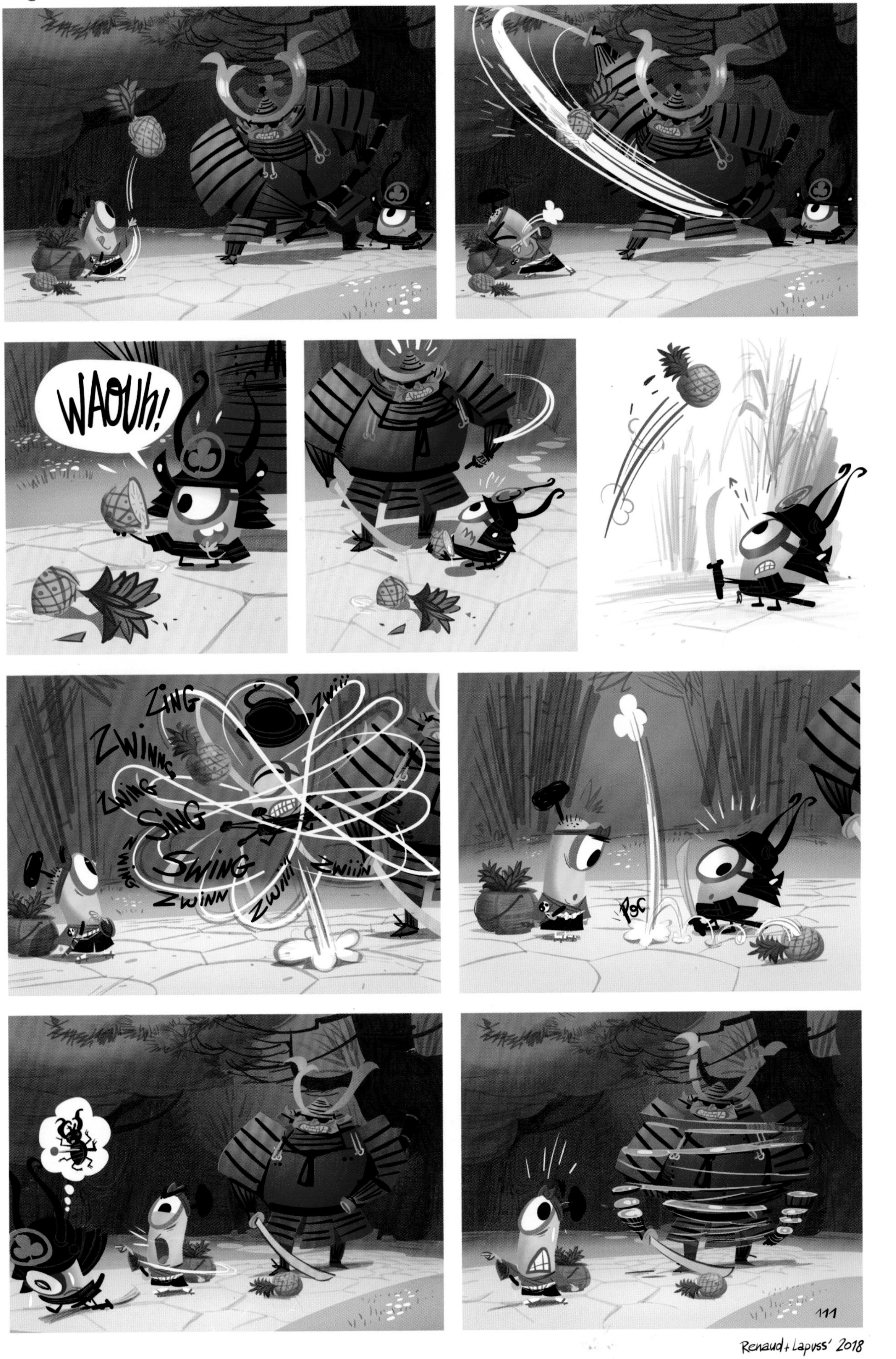
WAOUH!
ZING
ZWINNG
ZWiii
ZWING
SING
NWING
SWING
ZWiiiN
ZWINN
ZWiiii
POC

Renaud+Lapuss' 2018

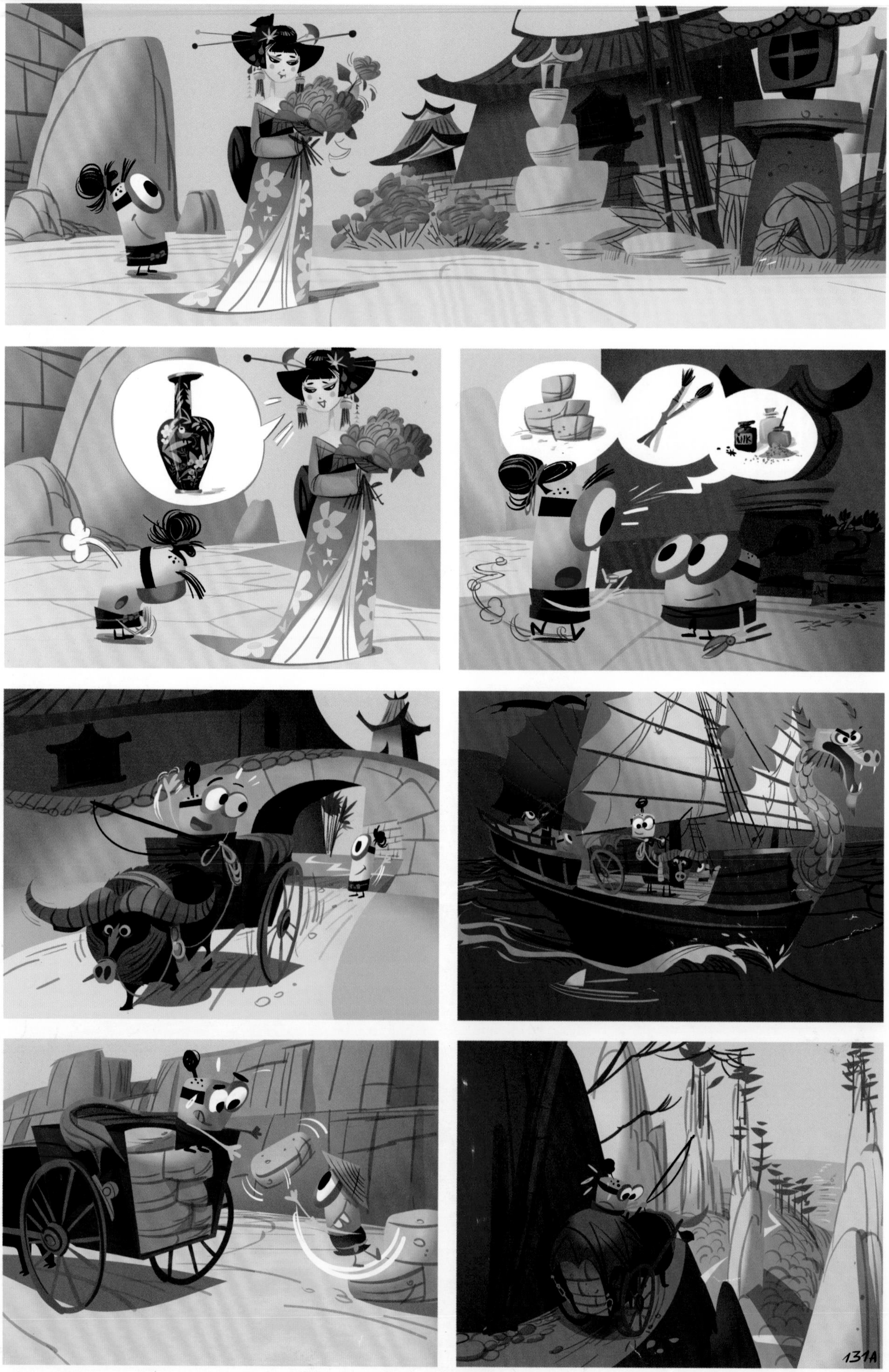
INK

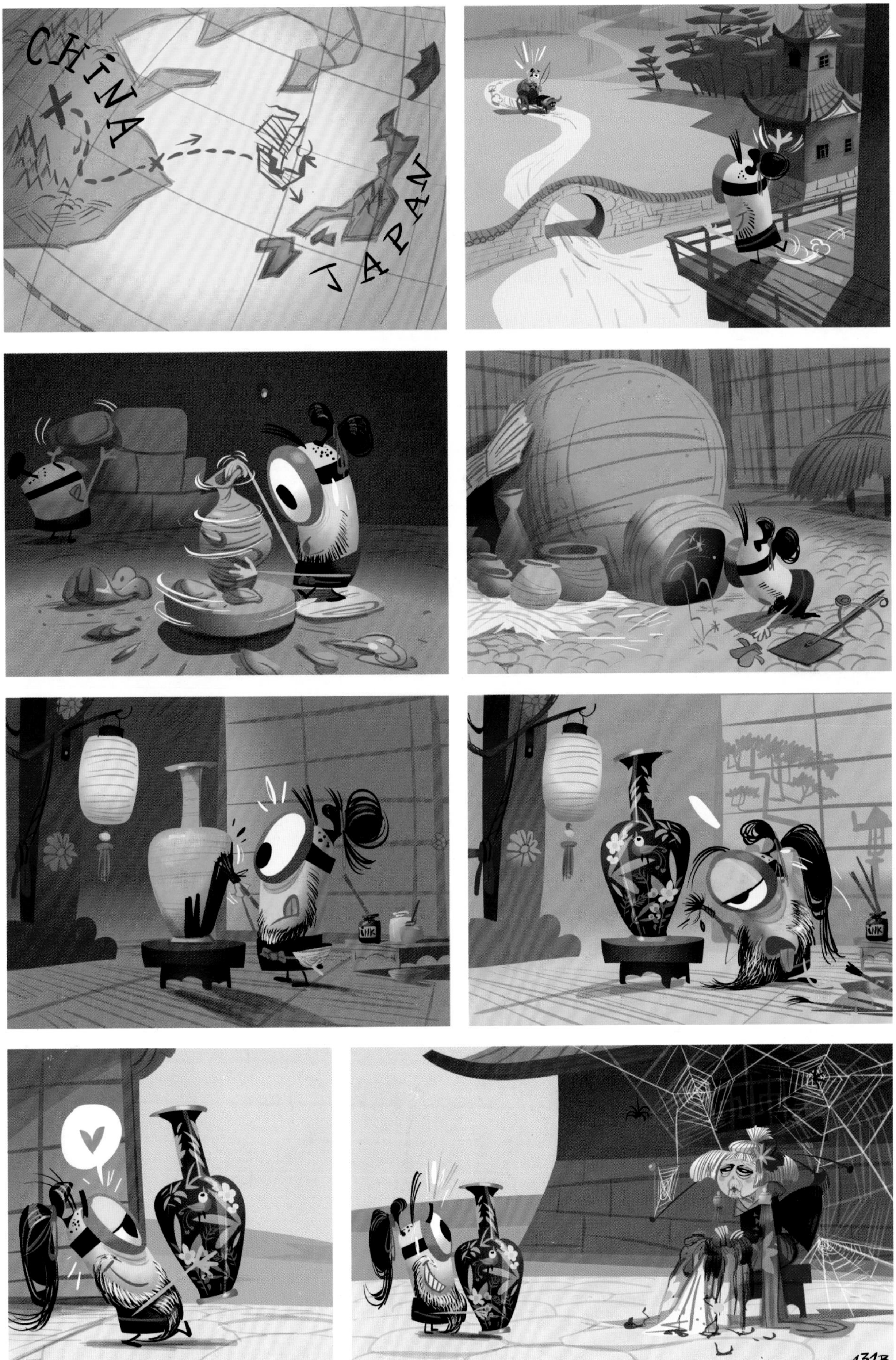
CHINA
JAPAN
INK
INK
131B

Renaud+Lapuss' 2018

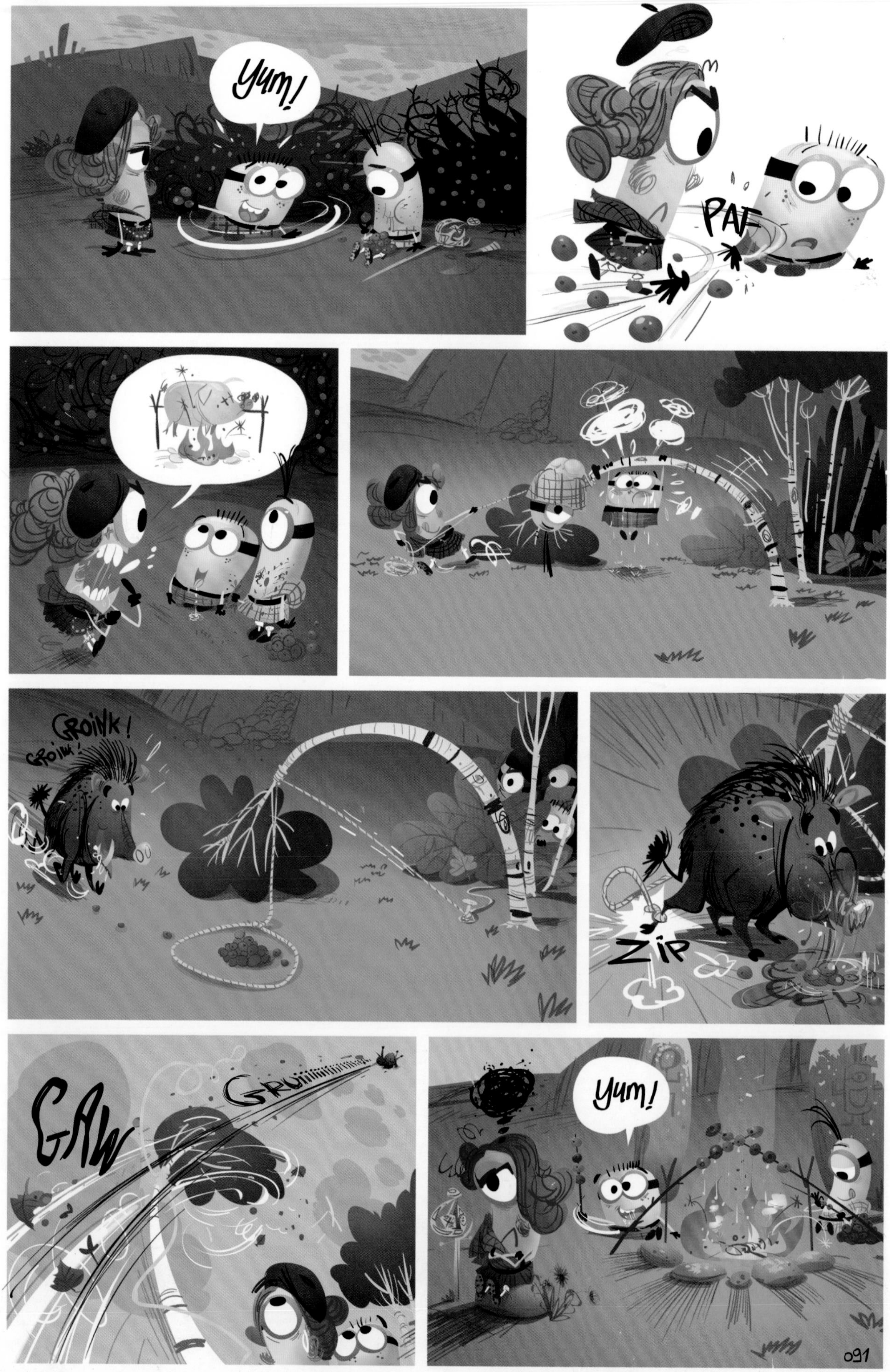

Yum!
PAF
GROINK!
GROINK!
ZIP
GAW
GRUiiiiiii
Yum!

Renaud + Lapuss' 2018

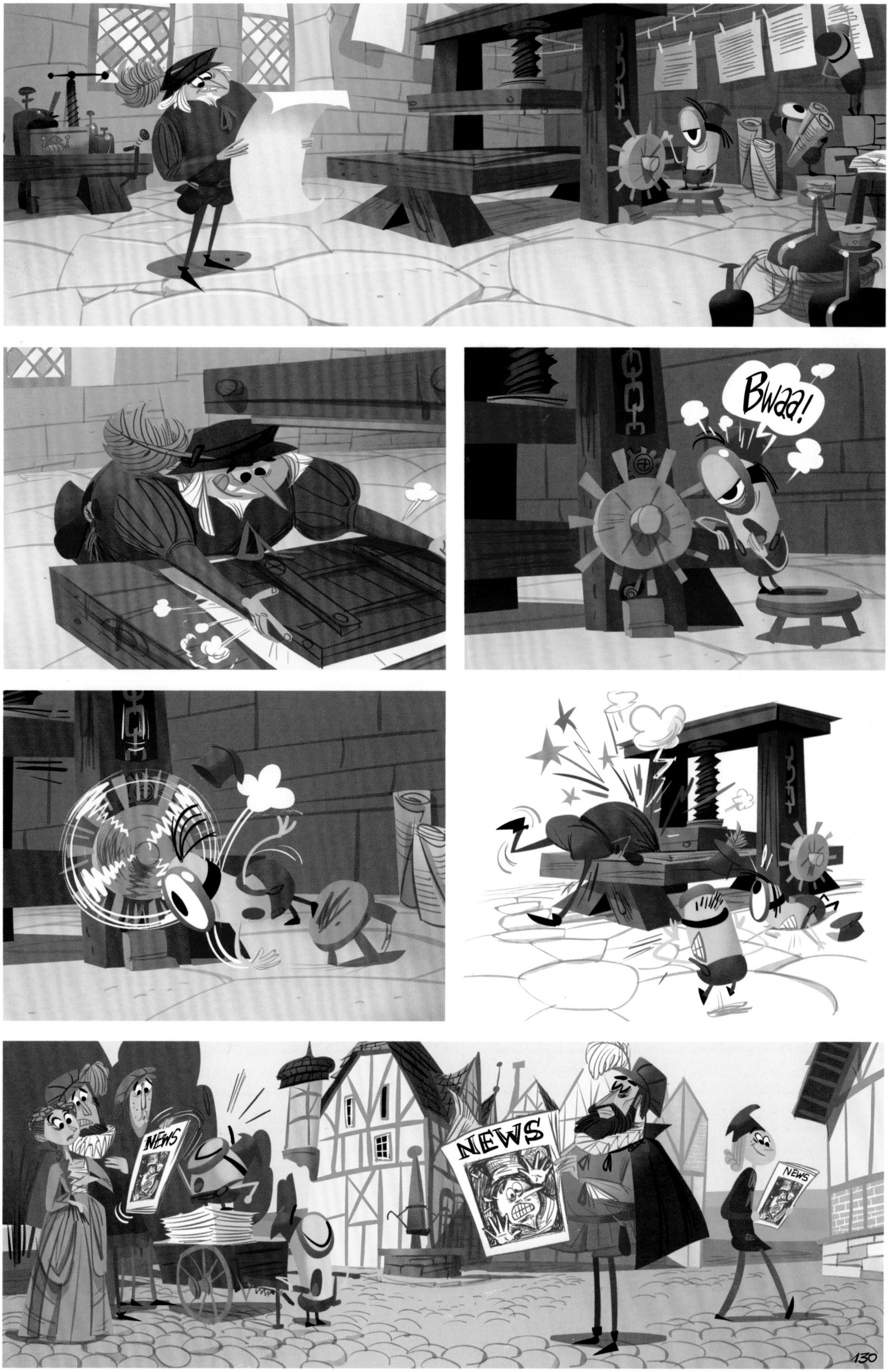
Bwaa!
NEWS
NEWS
NEWS

Renaud+Lapuss' 2018

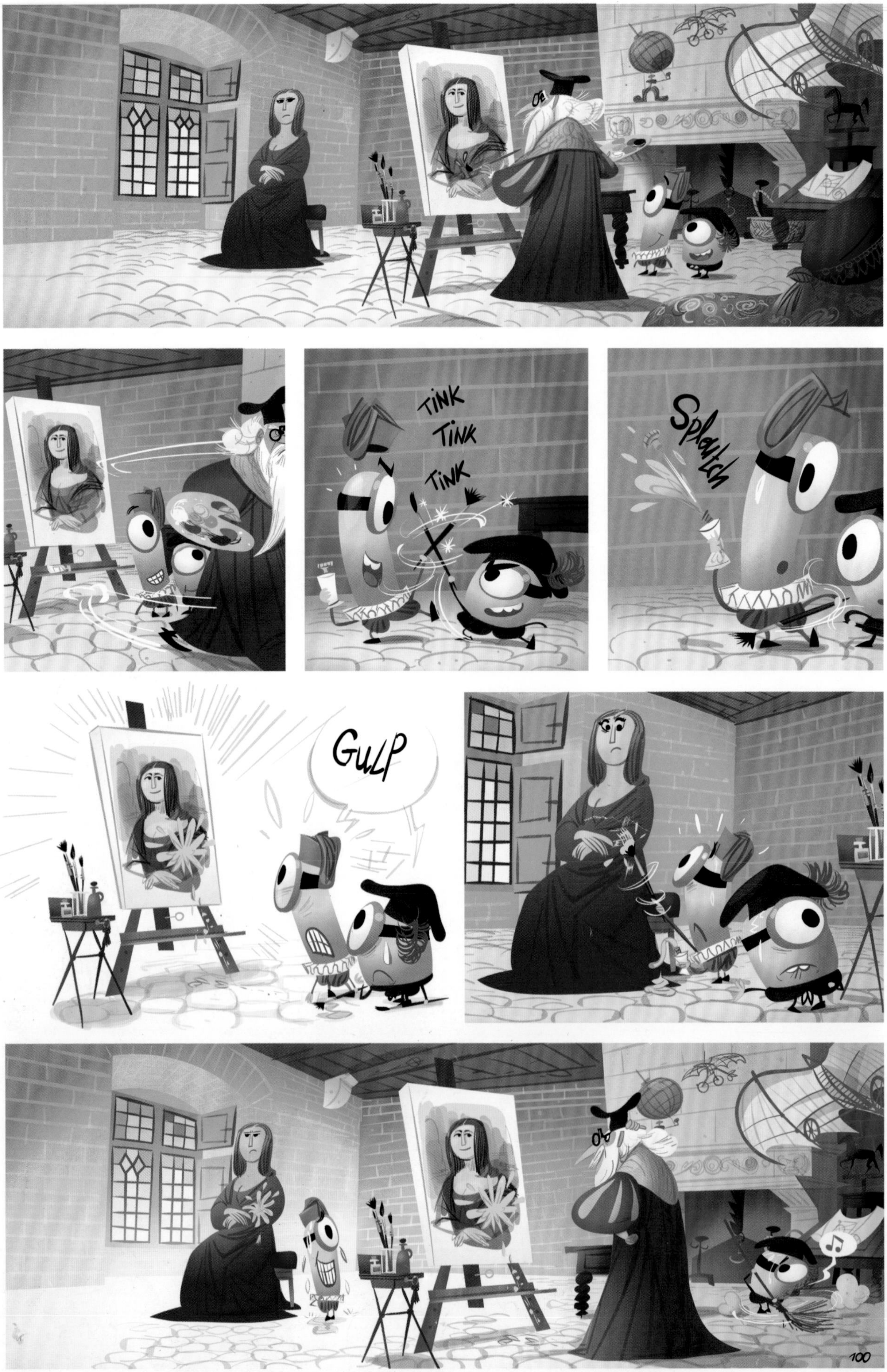
TINK
TINK
TINK
Splatch
GULP

Renaud+Lapuss' 2018

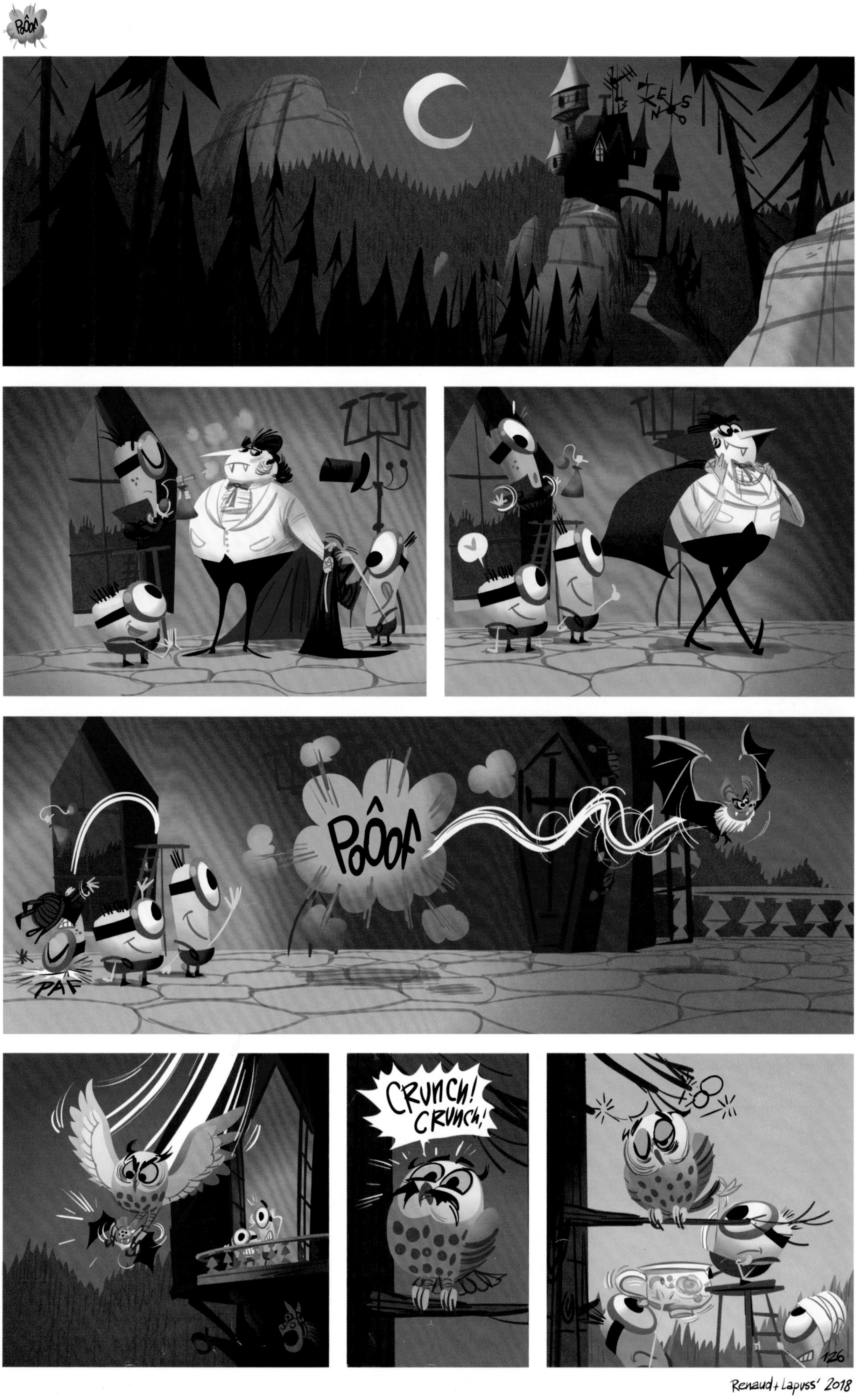

PoÔoF
PoÔoF
PAF
CRUNCH!
CRUNCH!
126

Renaud+Lapuss' 2018

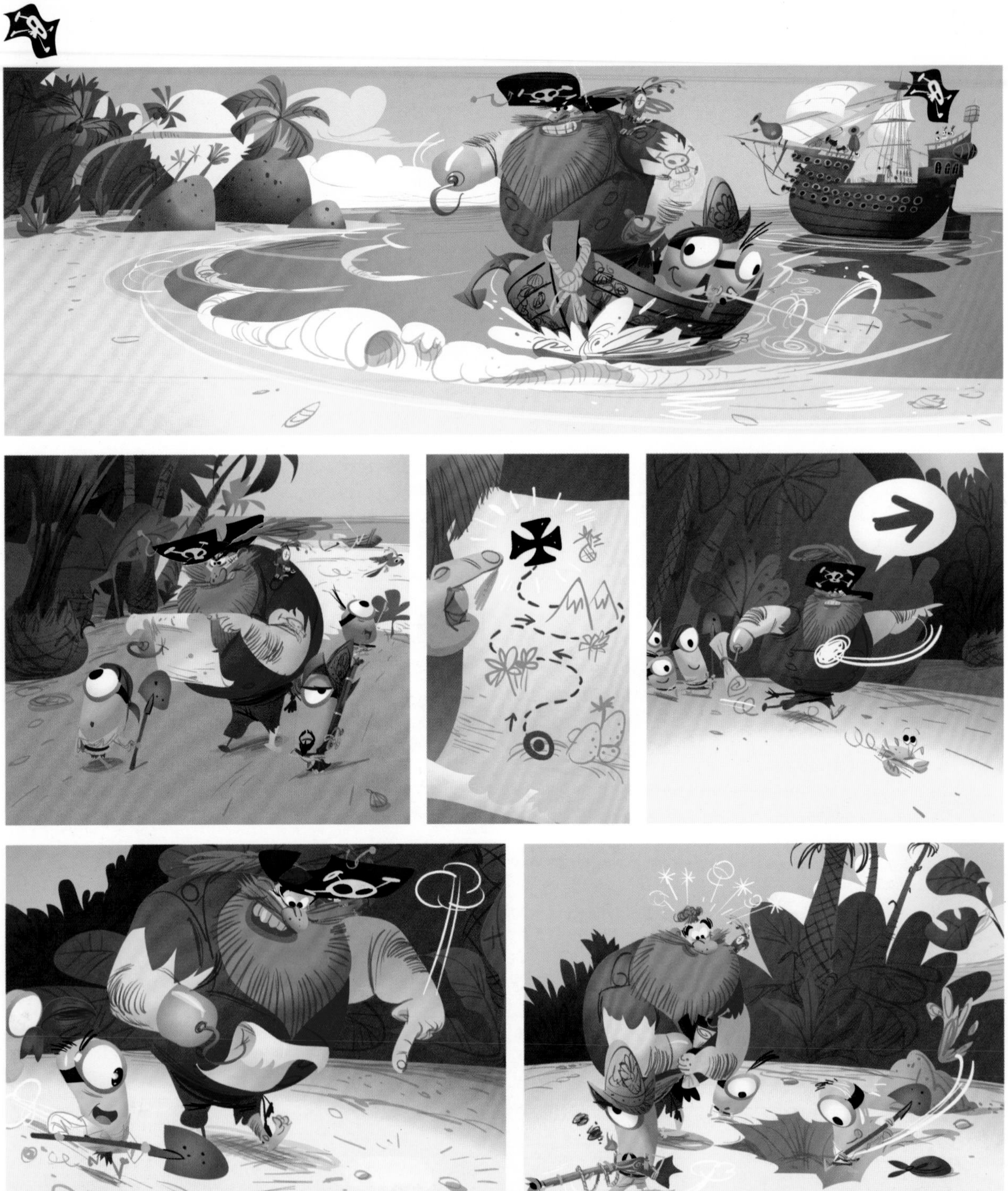
BING!
POW

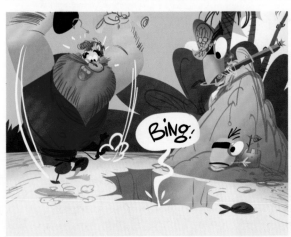

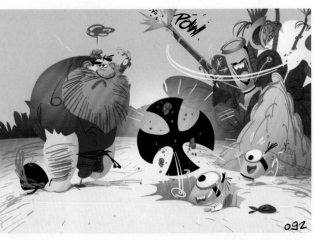

Renaud+Lapuss' 2018

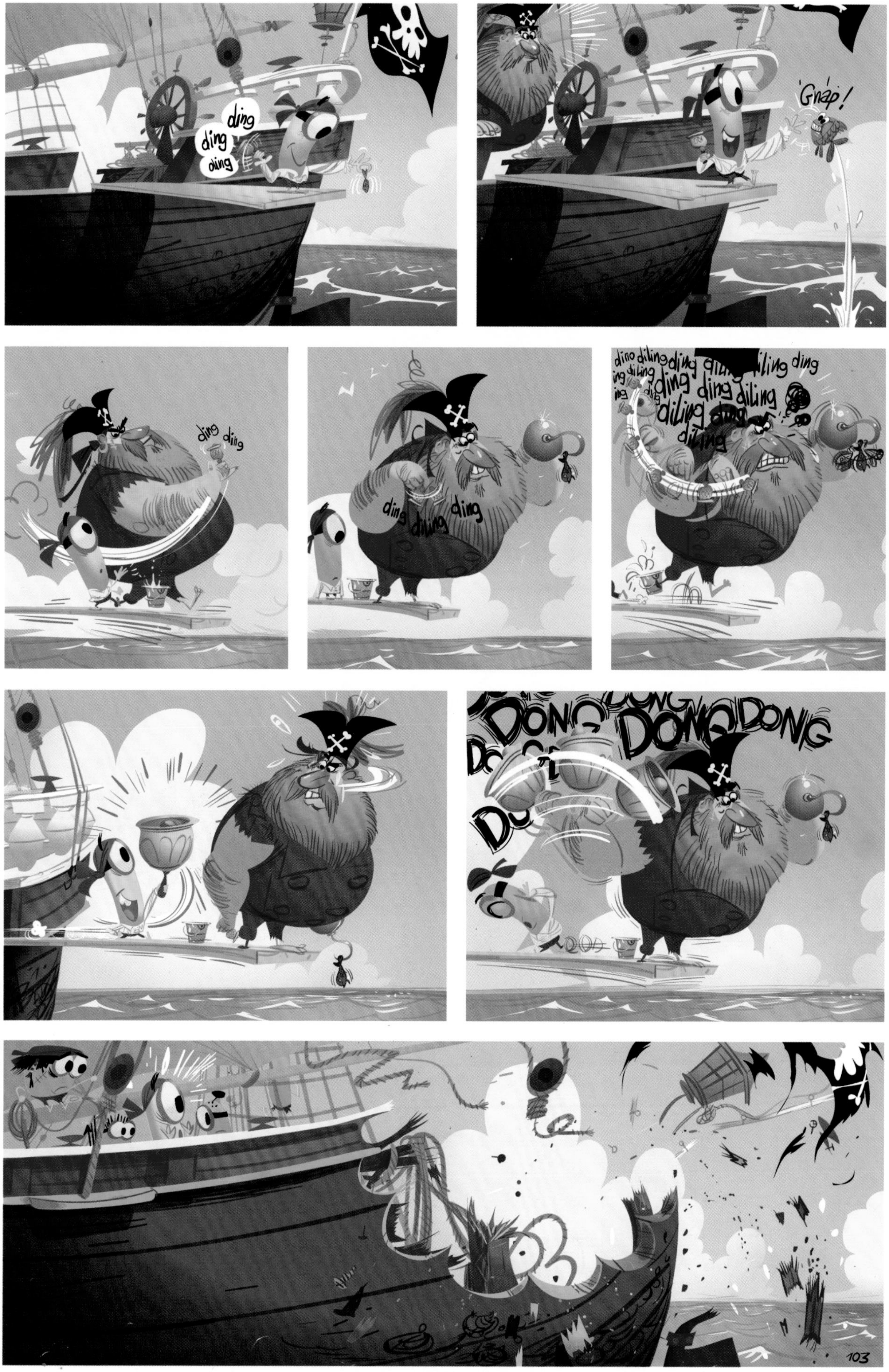
ding
ding
ding
'Gnap!
ding diling
ding diling ding
diling ding ding diling ding
ding diling
DONG DONG DONG DONG

Renaud+Lapuss' 2018

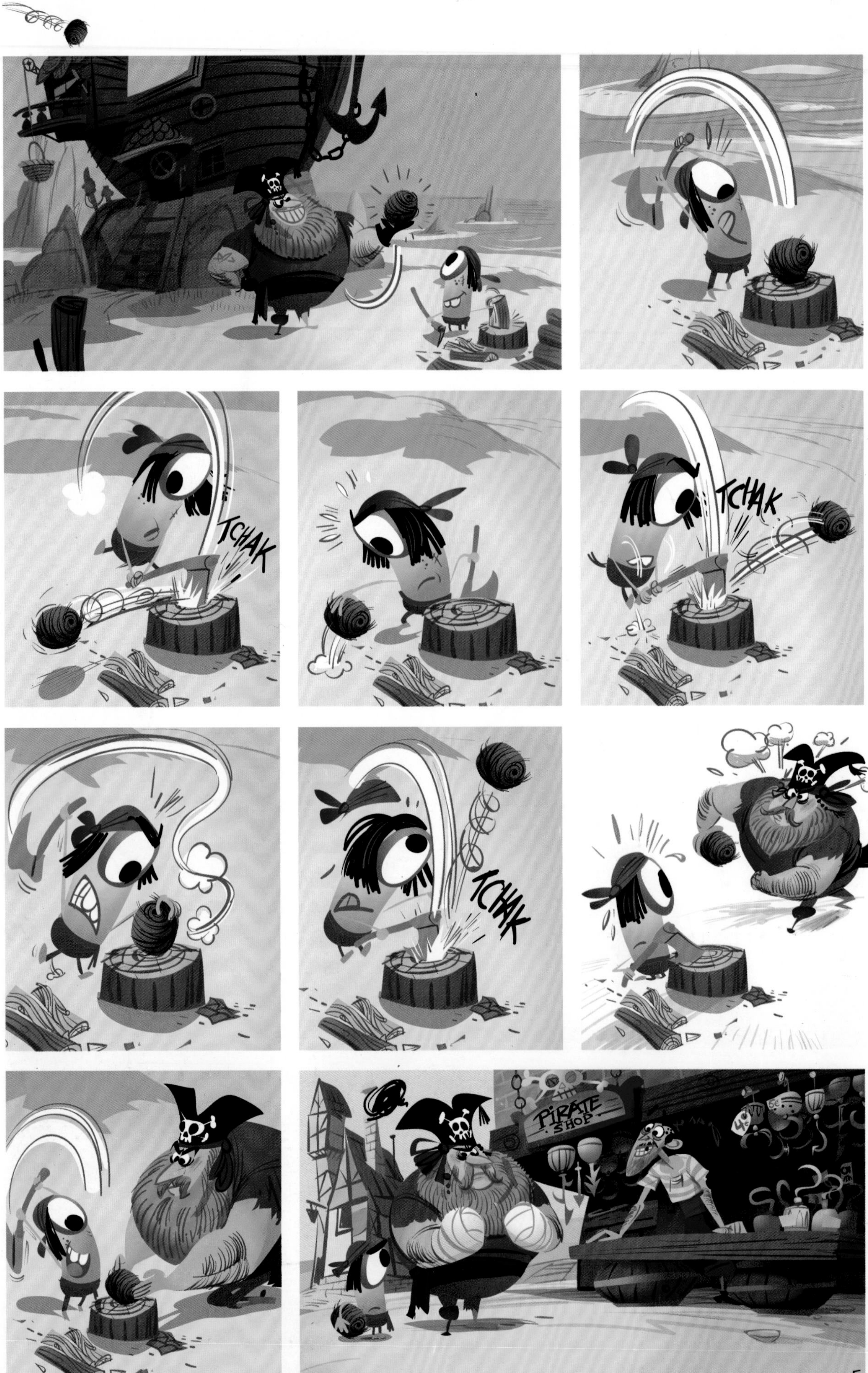
TCHAK
TCHAK
TCHAK
PIRATE SHOP

Renaud + Lapuss' 2018

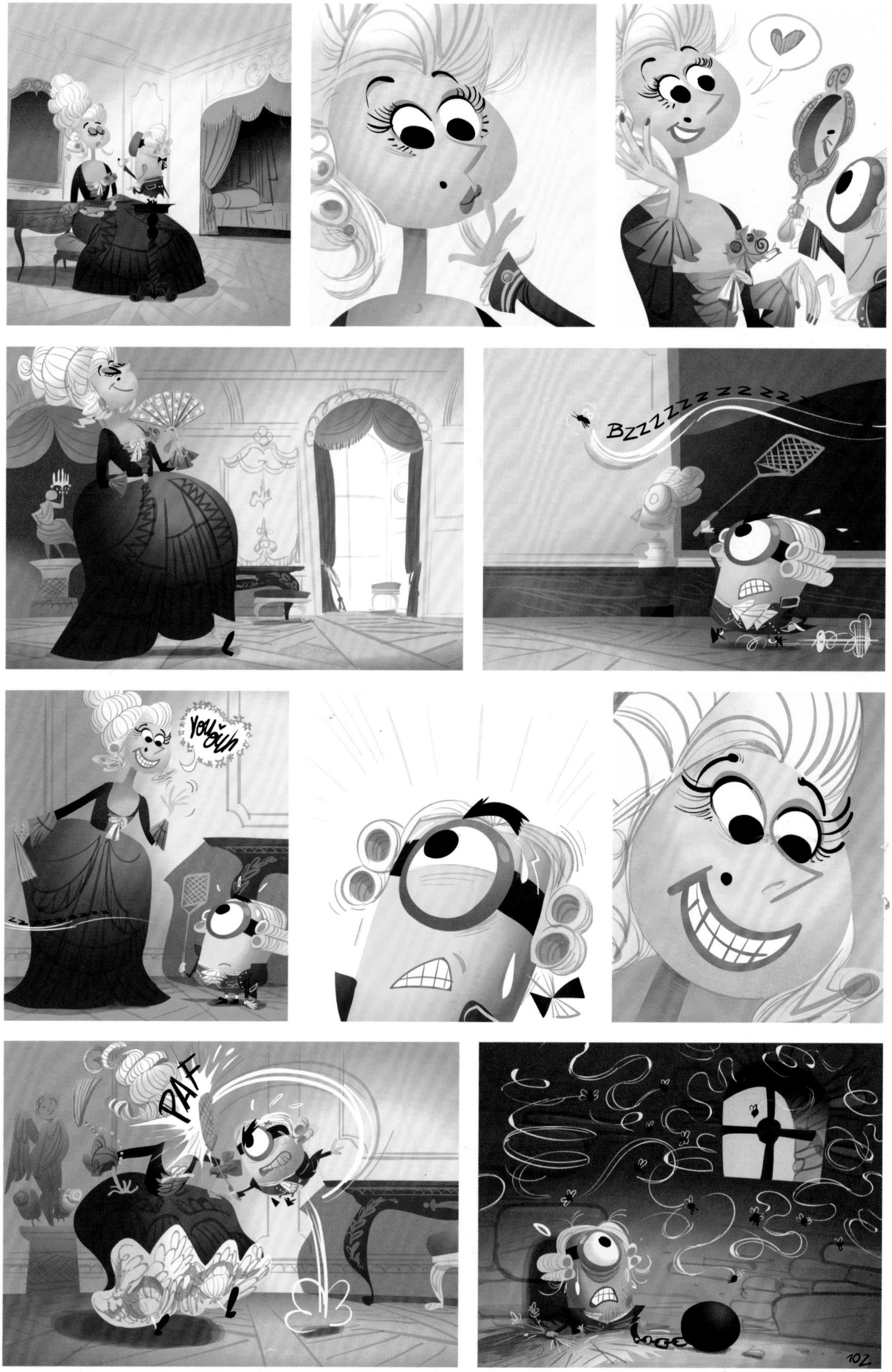
BZZZZZZZZZZZ
You ouh
PAF
102
Renaud+Lapuss' 2018

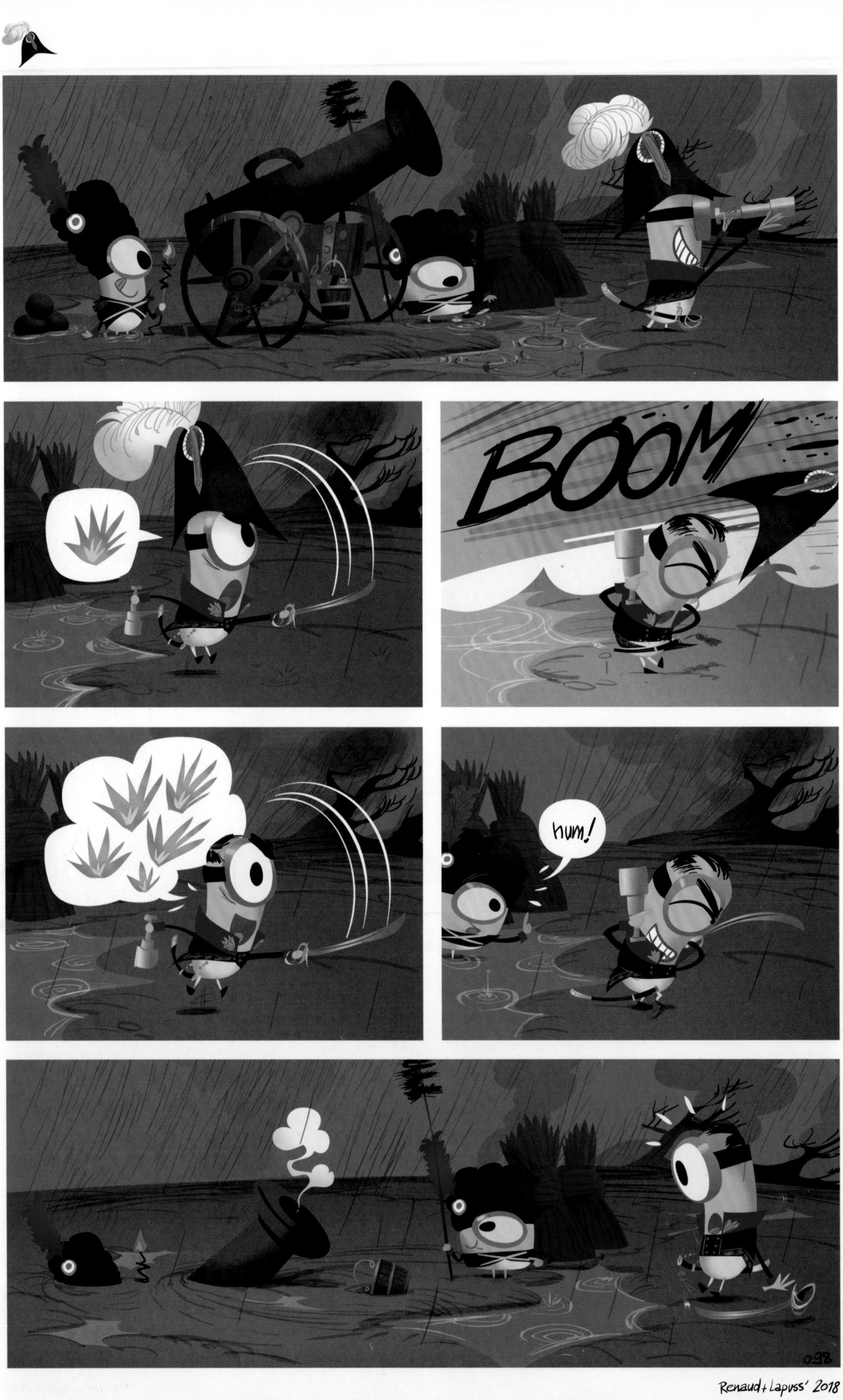
BOOM
hum!
098

Renaud+Lapuss' 2018

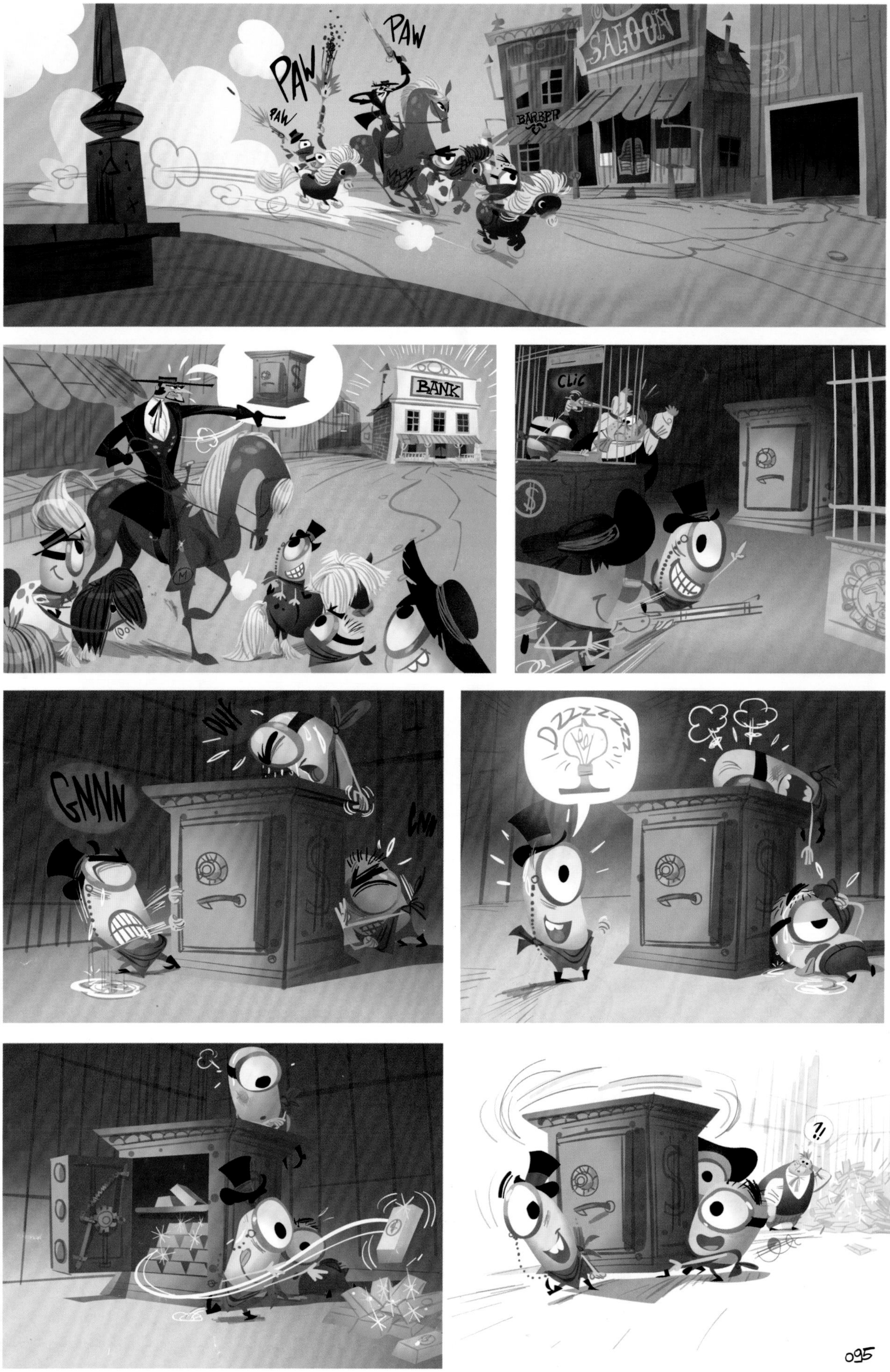
PAW
PAW
PAW
PAW
SALOON
BARBER
BANK
CLIC
GNNN
?!

Renaud + Lapuss' 2018

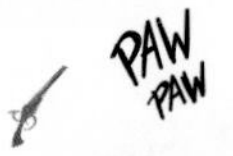
PAW
PAW

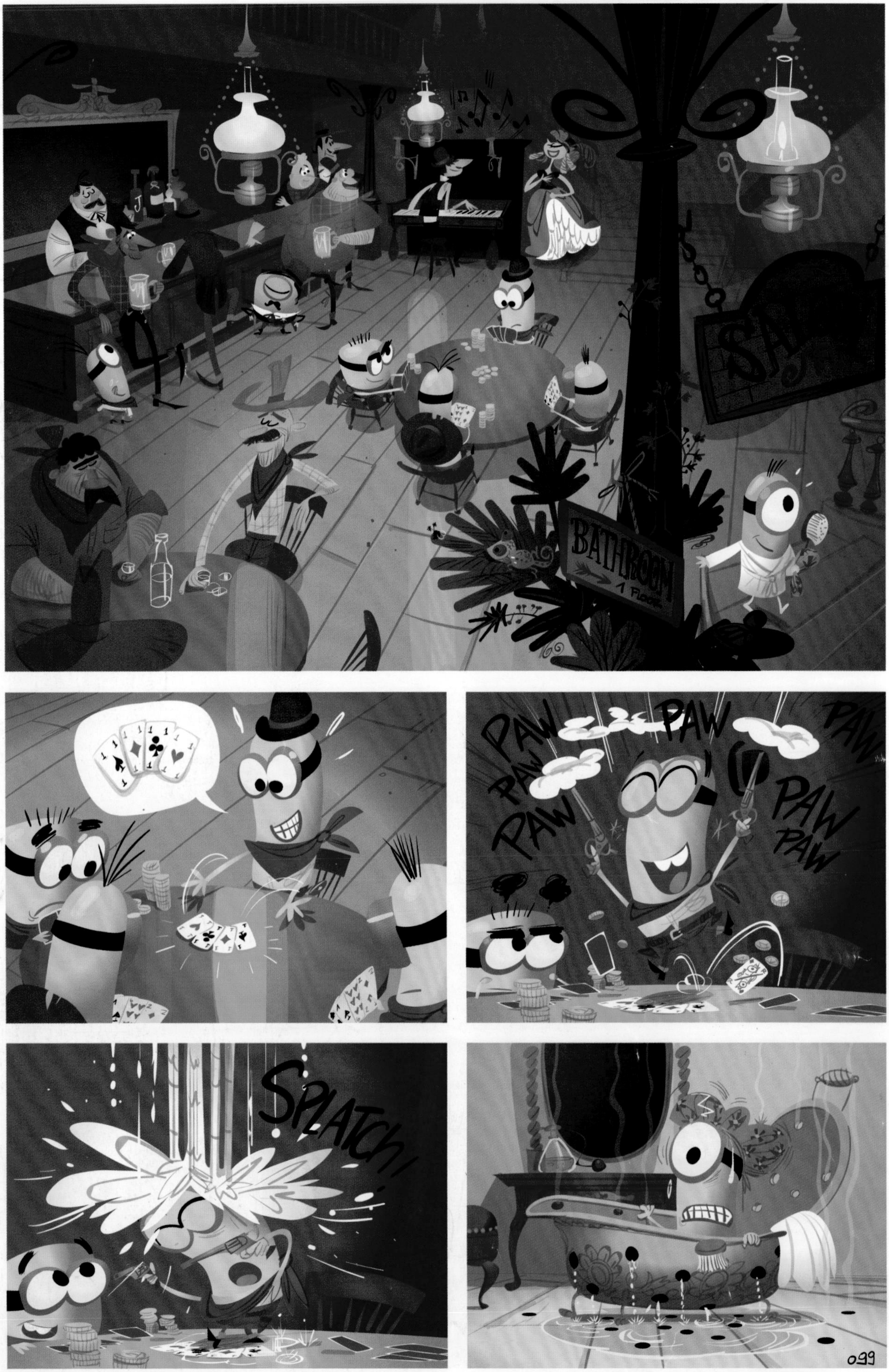
BATHROOM
1 Floor
PAW
PAW
PAW
PAW
PAW
PAW
PAW
PAW
SPLATCH!

Renaud+Lapuss' 2018

BBRROOOOOOOOOOOOOOOOOOOOO

Renaud + Lapuss' 2018

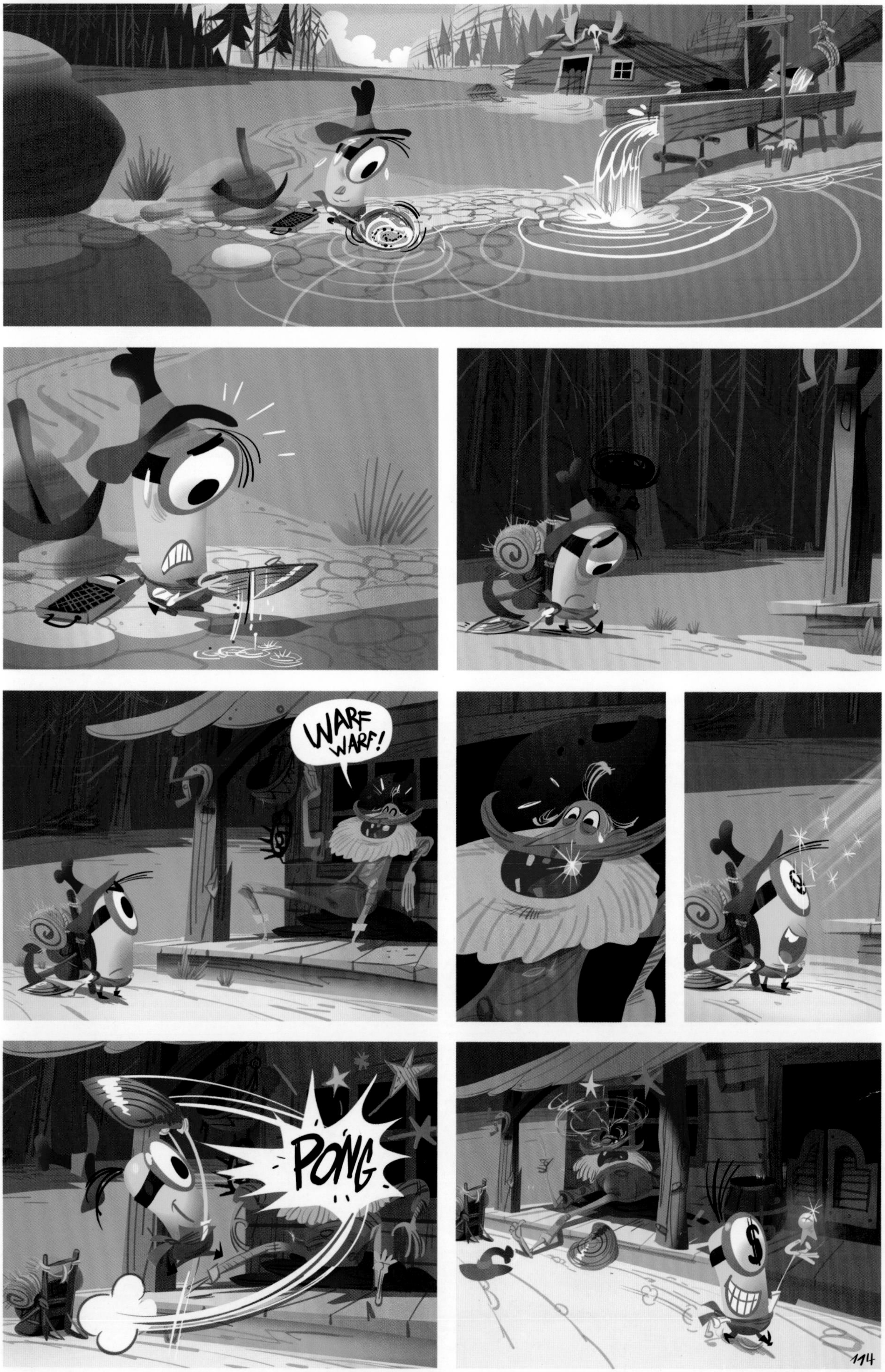
WARF WARF!
PONG

Renaud + Lapuss' 2018

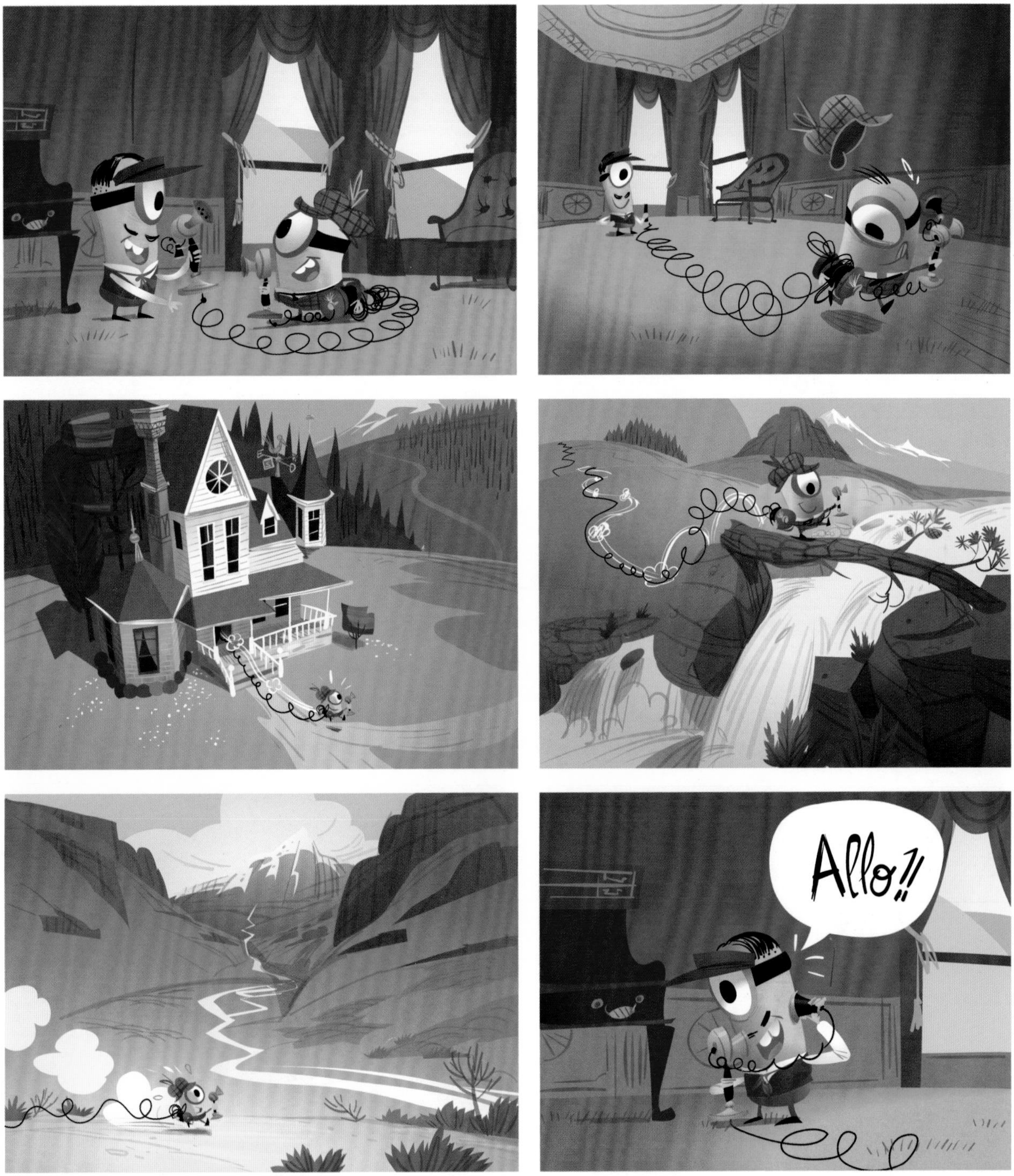
Allo!!
Allo!

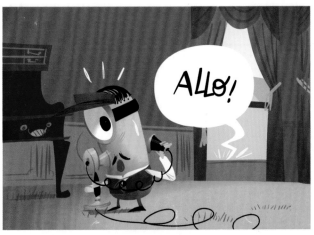

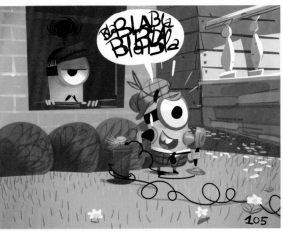

Renaud+Lapuss' 2018

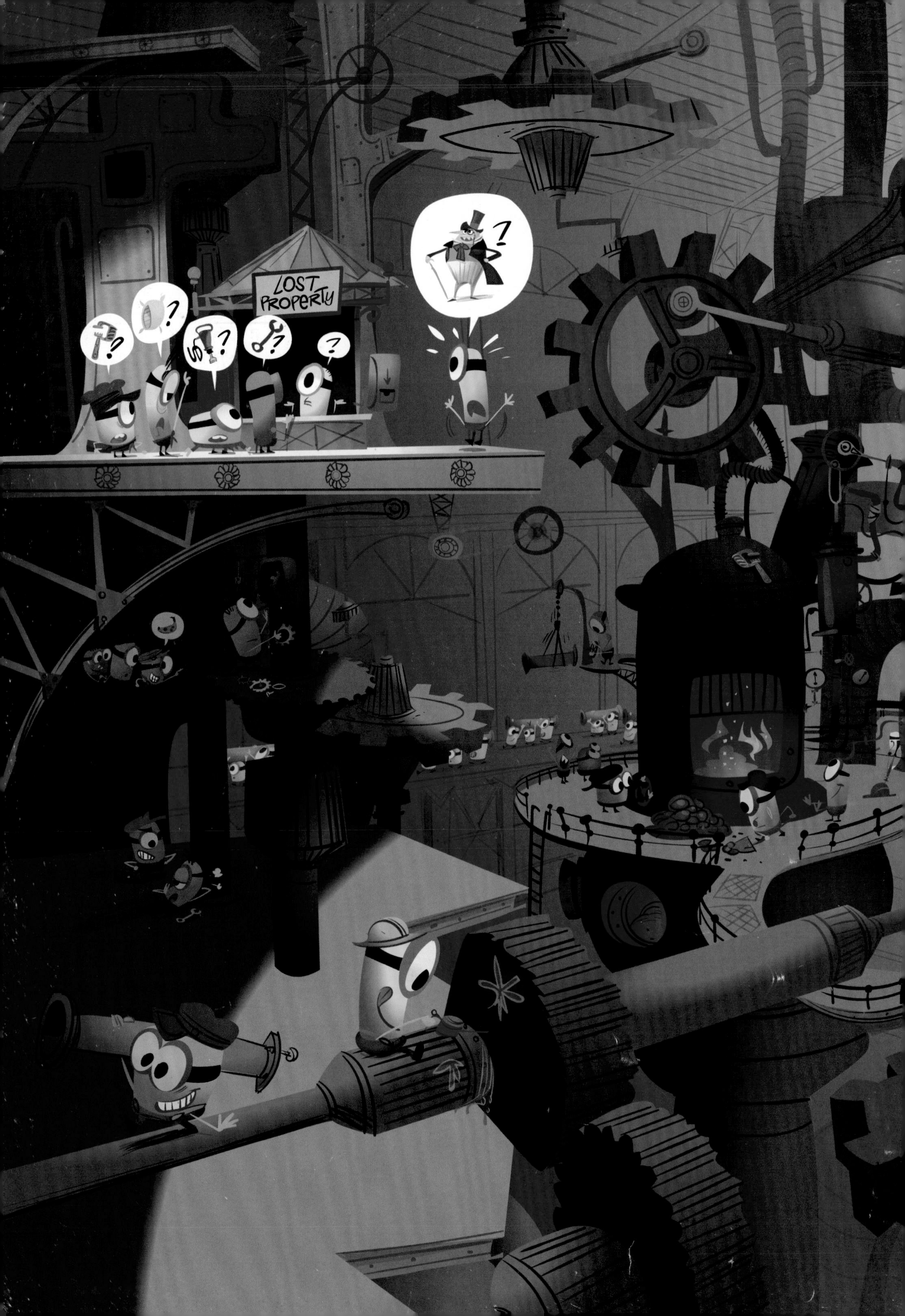

LOST PROPERTY

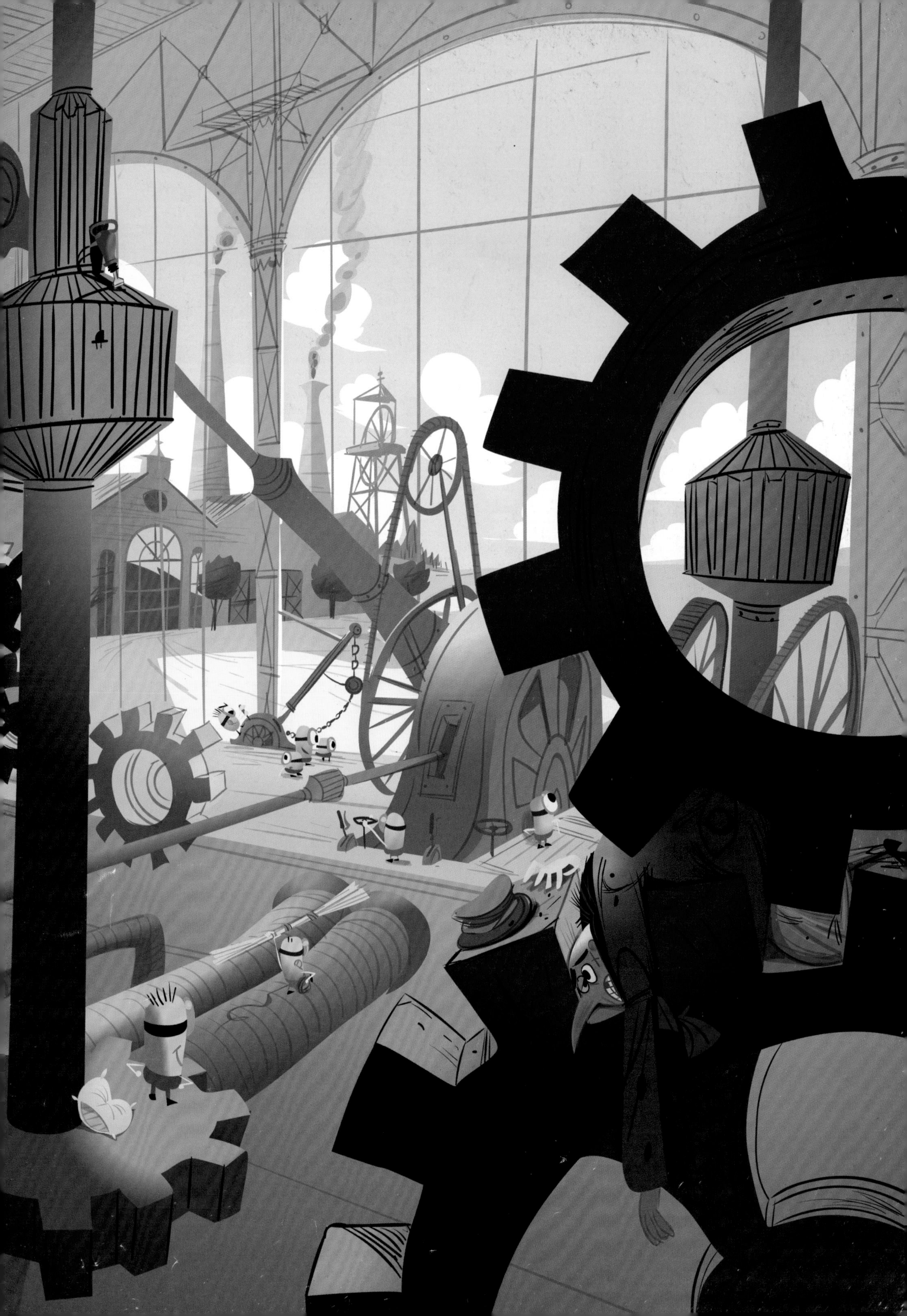

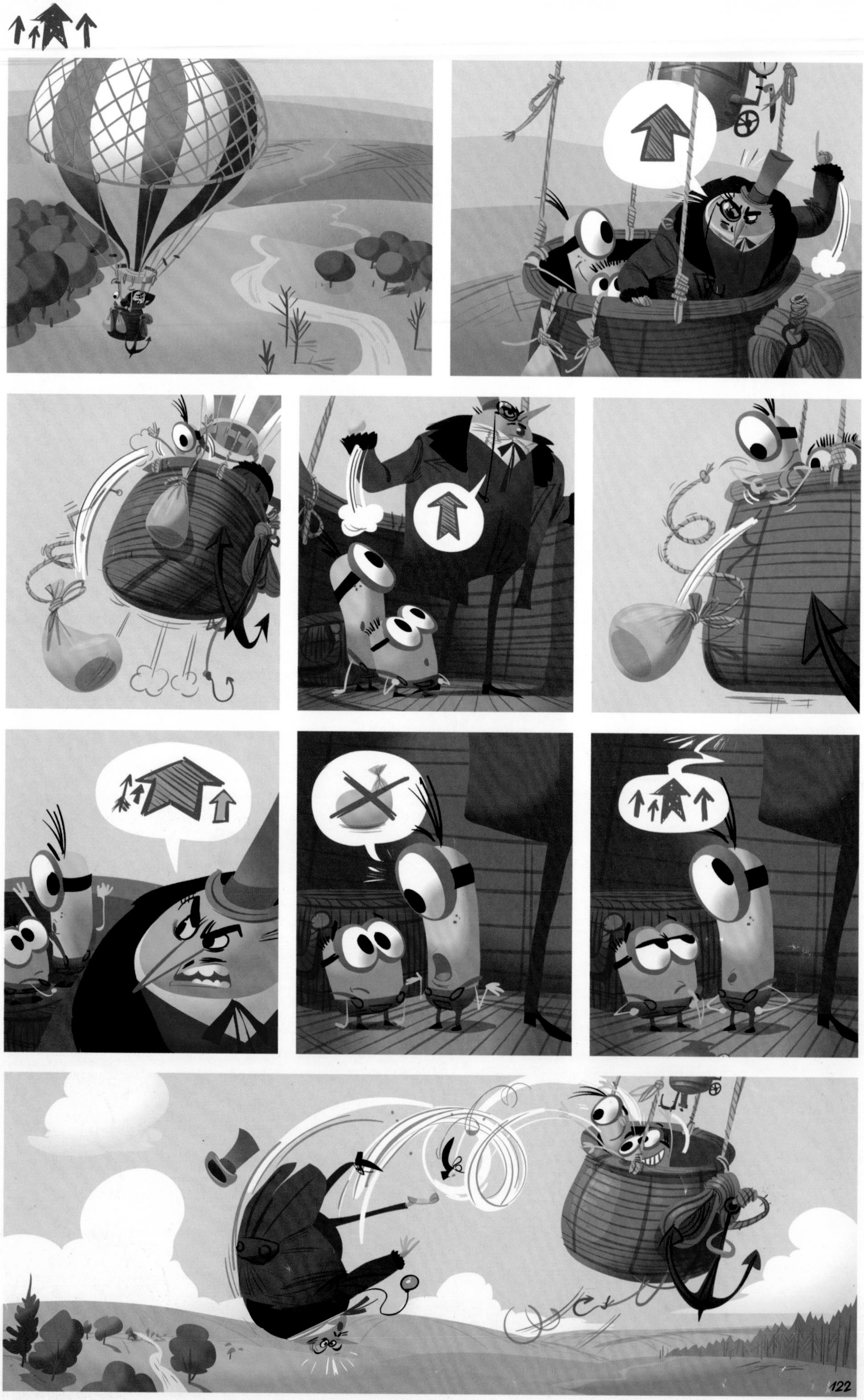
122

Renaud+Lapuss' 2018

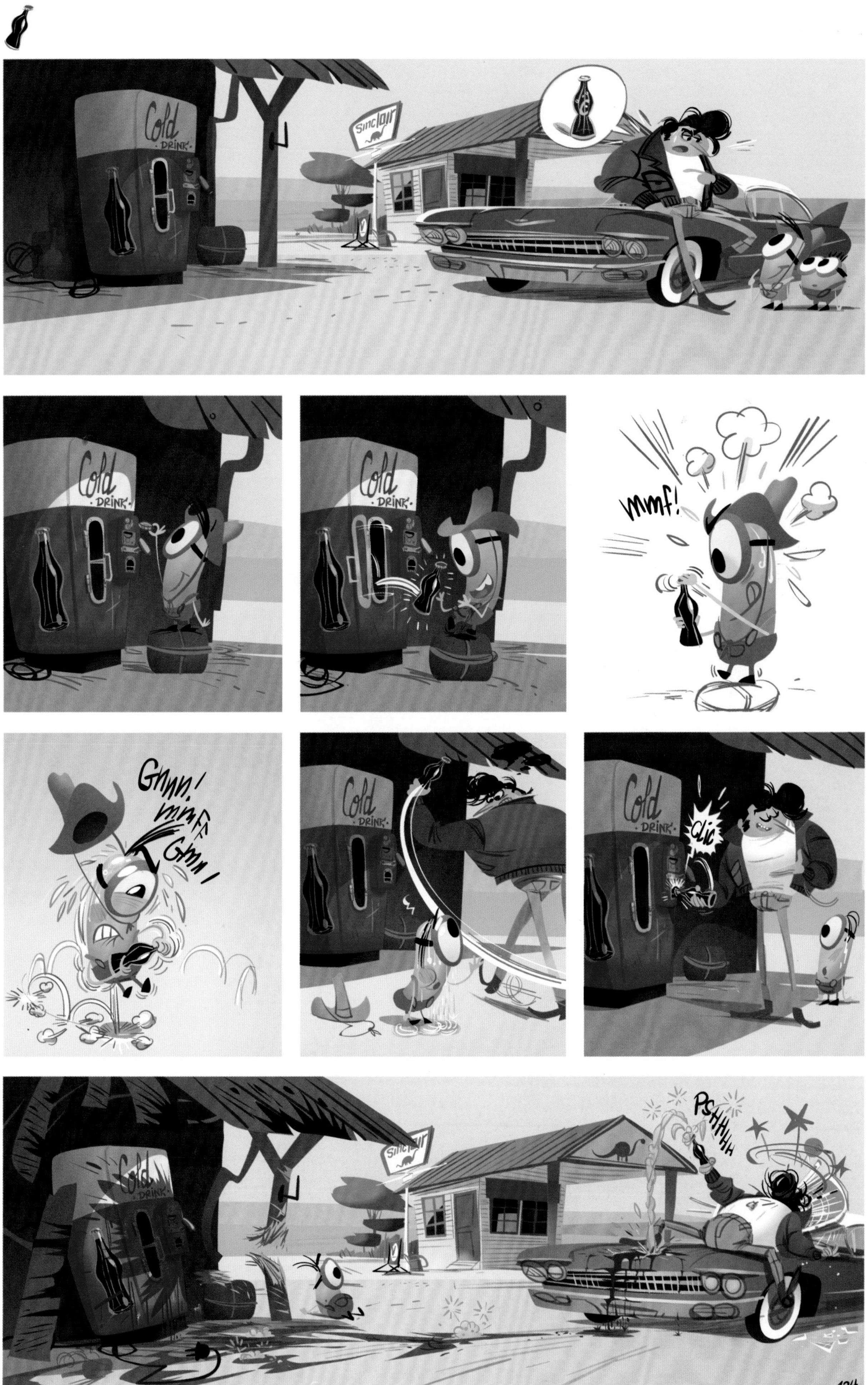
Cold DRINK
Sinclair
Cold DRINK
Cold DRINK
mmf!
Gnnn!
mmff
Gmn!
Cold DRINK
Cold DRINK
Clic
Cold DRINK
Sinclair
PSHHHH
124

Renaud+Lapuss' 2018

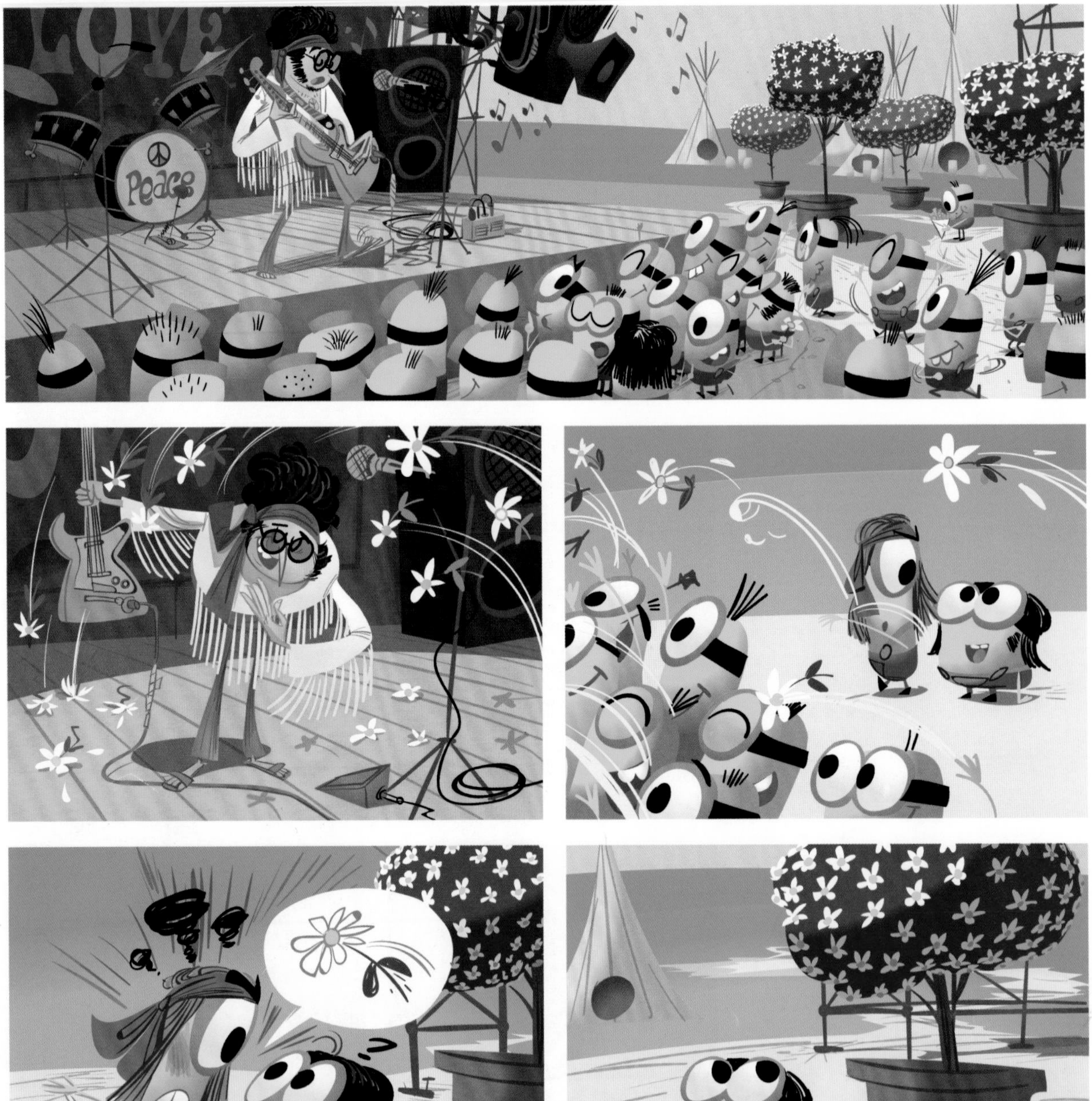
LOVE
Peace

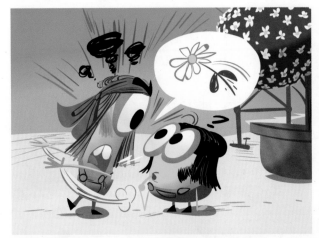

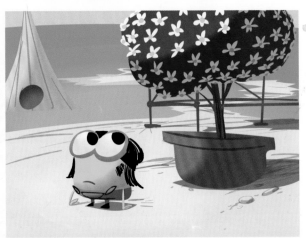

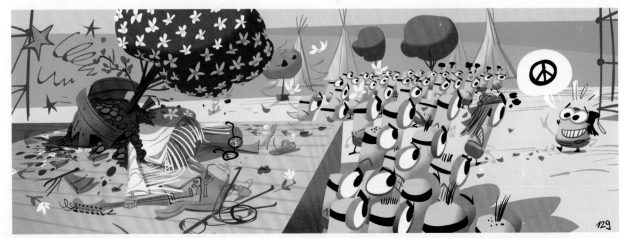

Renaud+Lapuss' 2018

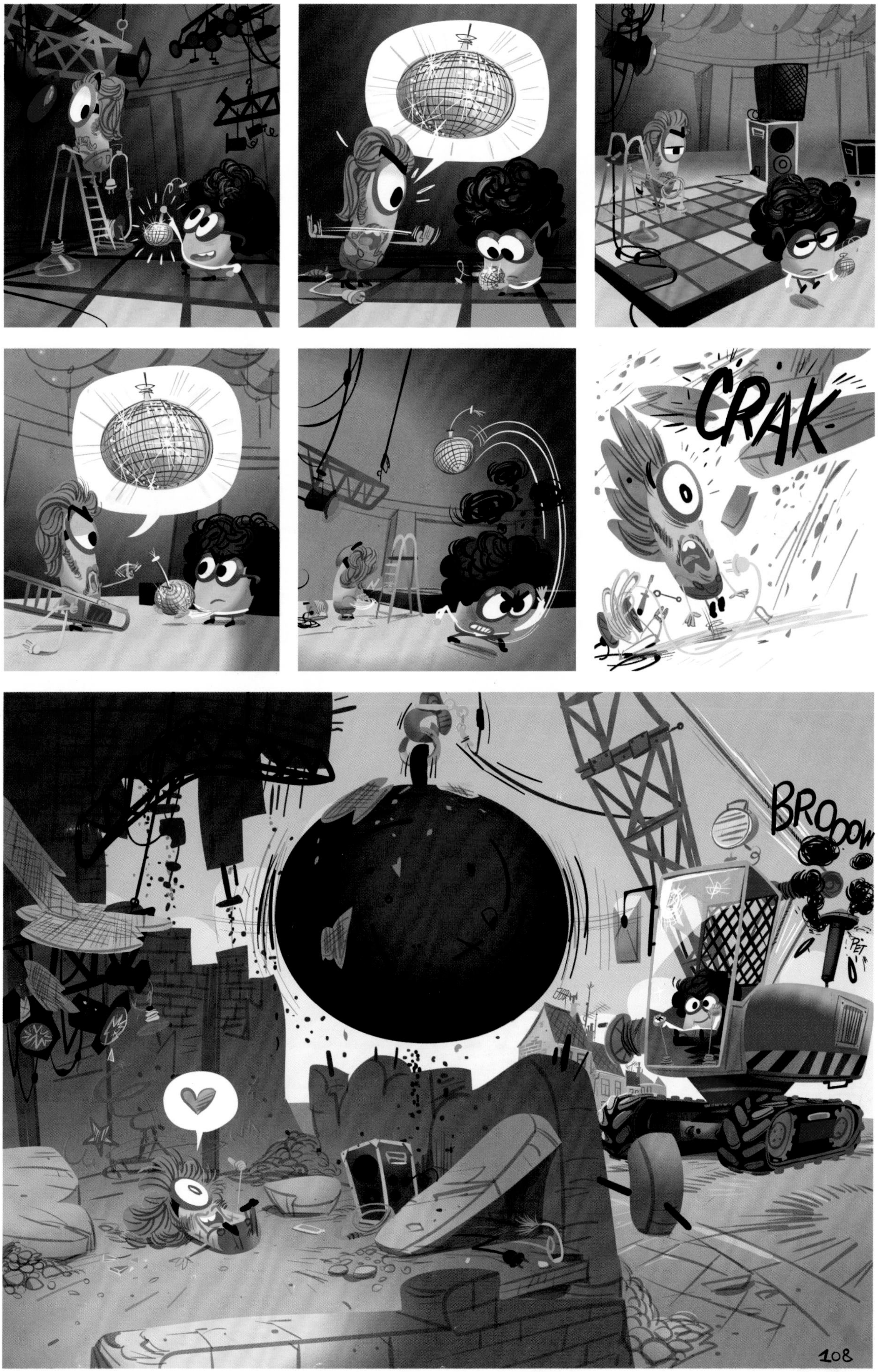
CRAK
BROOOW
PET

Renaud+Lapuss' 2018

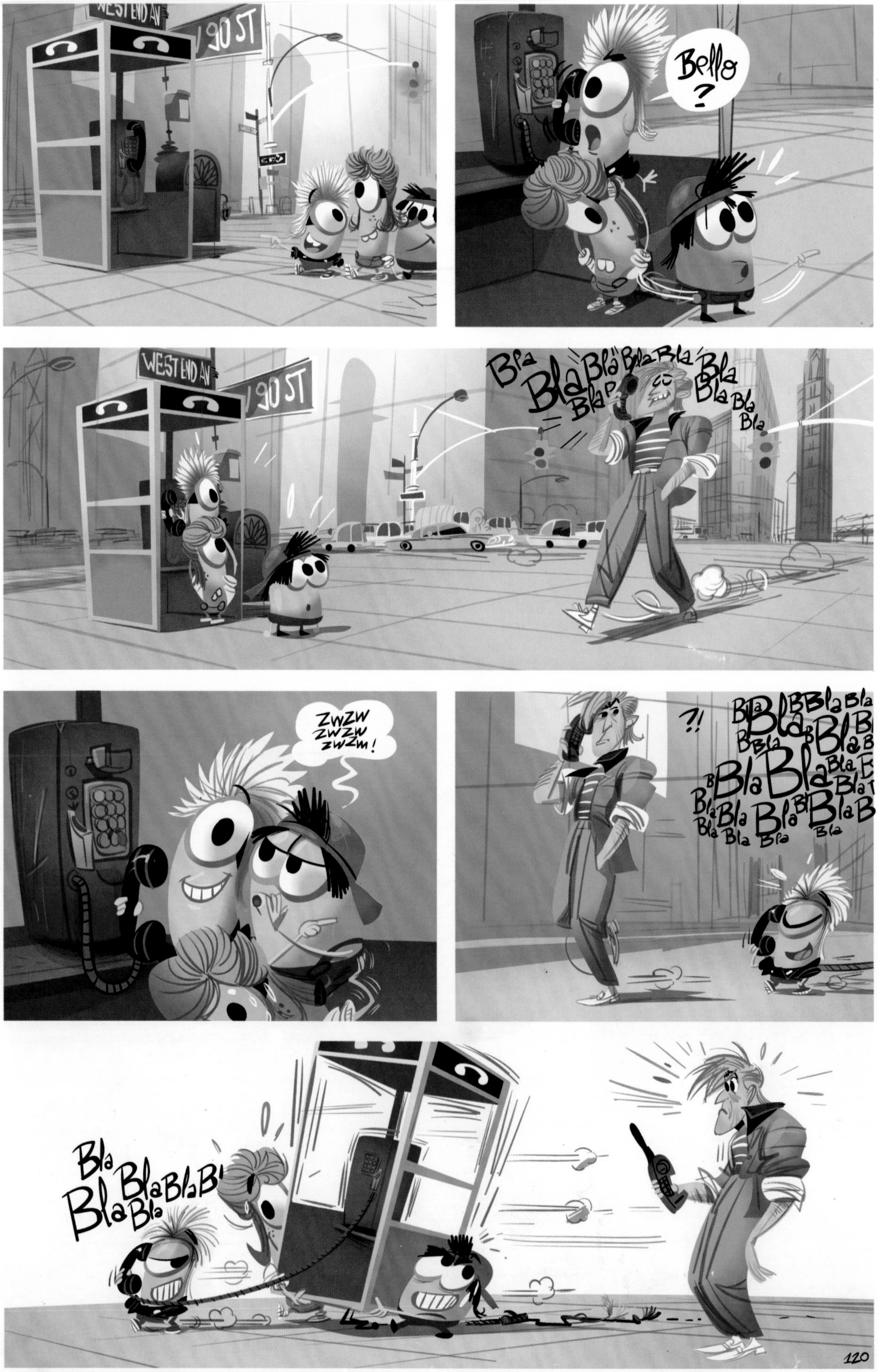
WEST END AV
90 ST
Bello ?
WEST END AV
90 ST
Bla Bla Bla Bla Bla Bla Bla Bla Bla Bla
ZWZW ZWZW ZWZW!
?!
Bla Bla Bla Bla Bla Bla Bla Bla Bla Bla Bla Bla Bla Bla Bla Bla
Bla Bla Bla Bla Bla Bla

Renaud + Lapuss' 2018

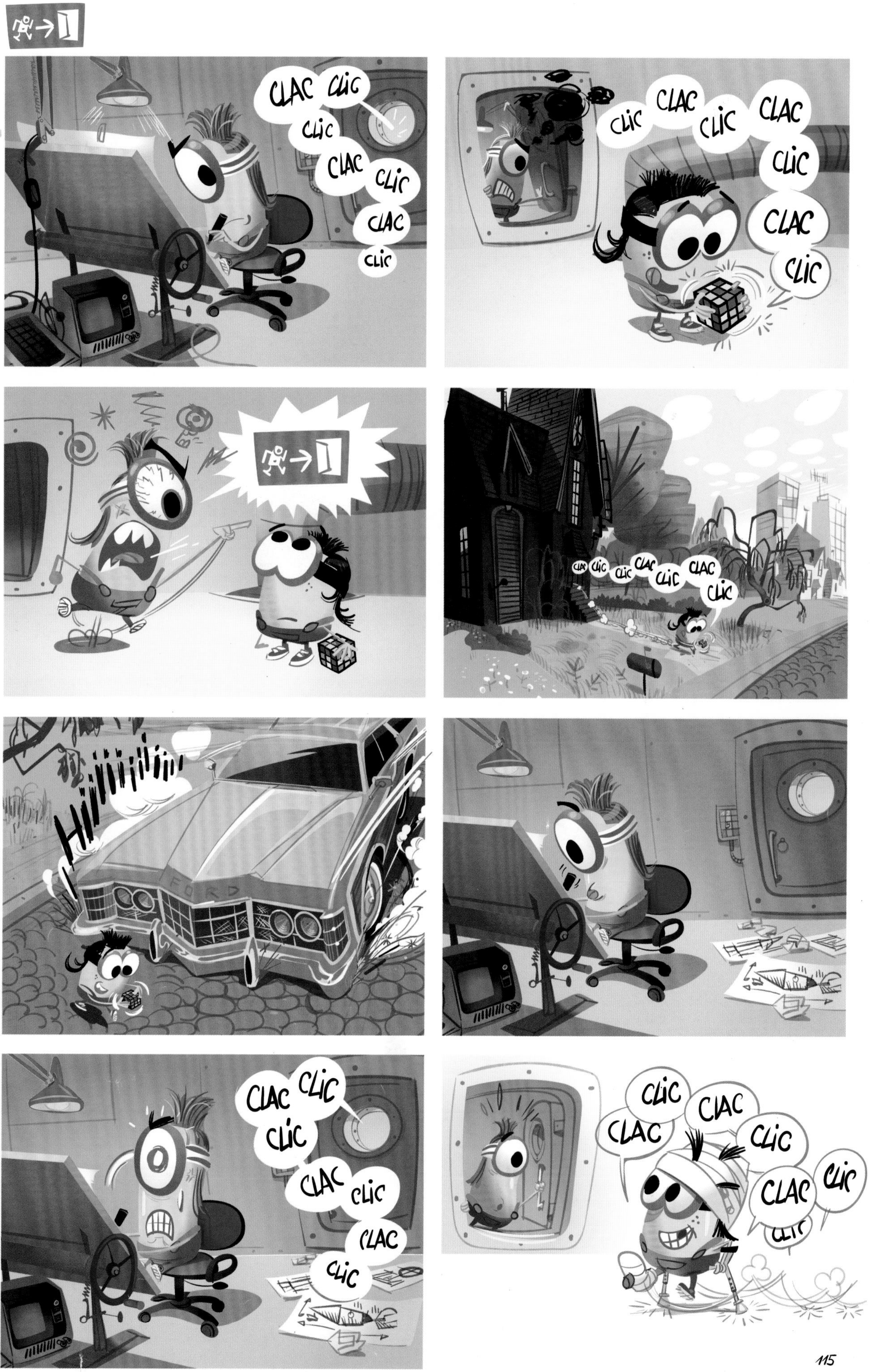
CLAC
CLIC
CLIC
CLAC
CLIC
CLAC
CLIC
CLIC
CLAC
CLIC
CLAC
CLIC
CLAC
CLIC
CLAC
CLIC
CLIC
CLAC
CLIC
CLAC
CLIC
Hiiiiiiiiiiii
FORD
CLAC
CLIC
CLIC
CLAC
CLIC
CLAC
CLIC
CLIC
CLAC
CLAC
CLIC
CLAC
CLIC

Renaud+ Lapuss' 2018

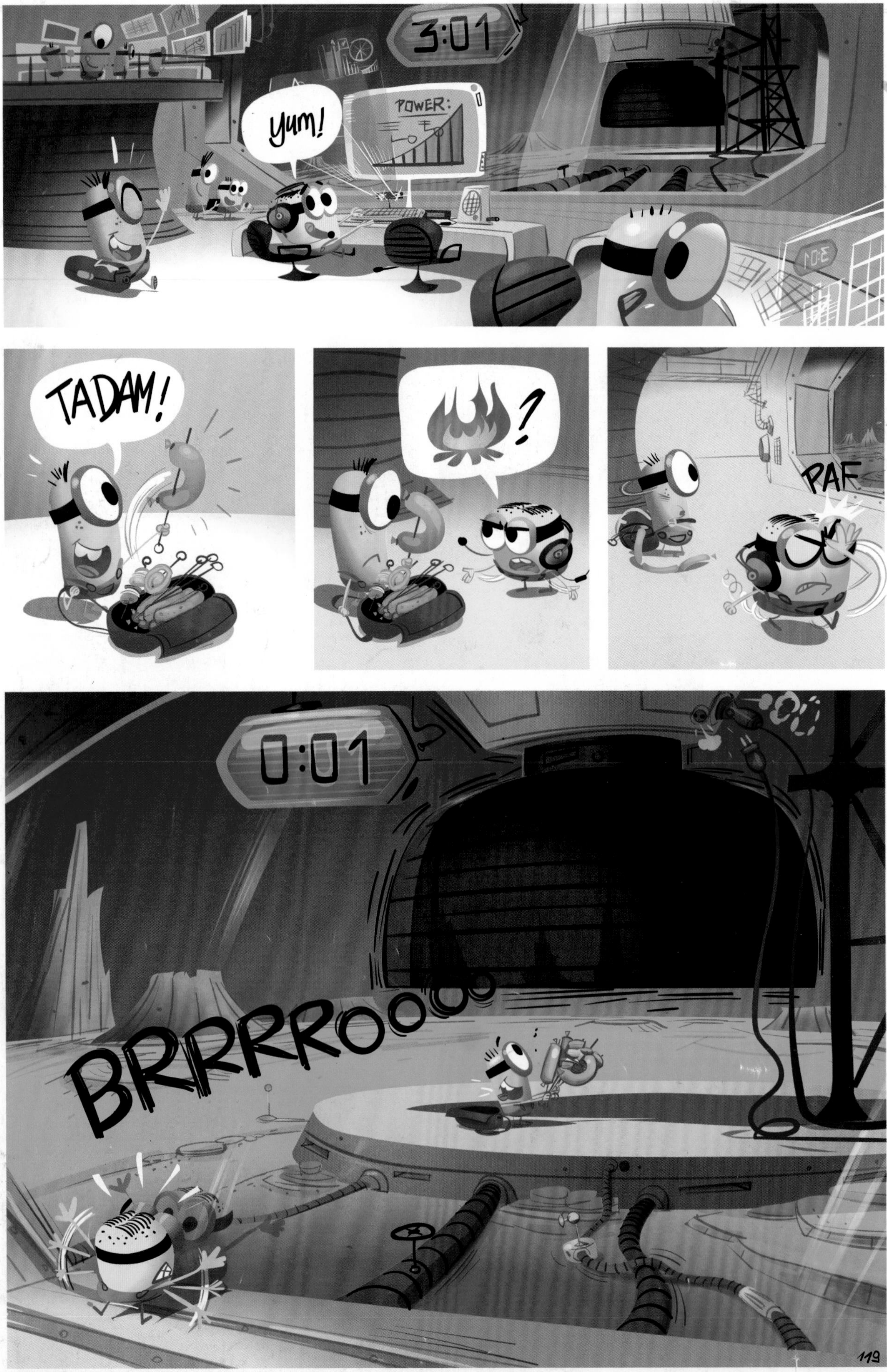
3:01
POWER:
YUM!
TADAM!
?
PAF
0:01
BRRRROOOOO

Renaud+Lapuss' 2018

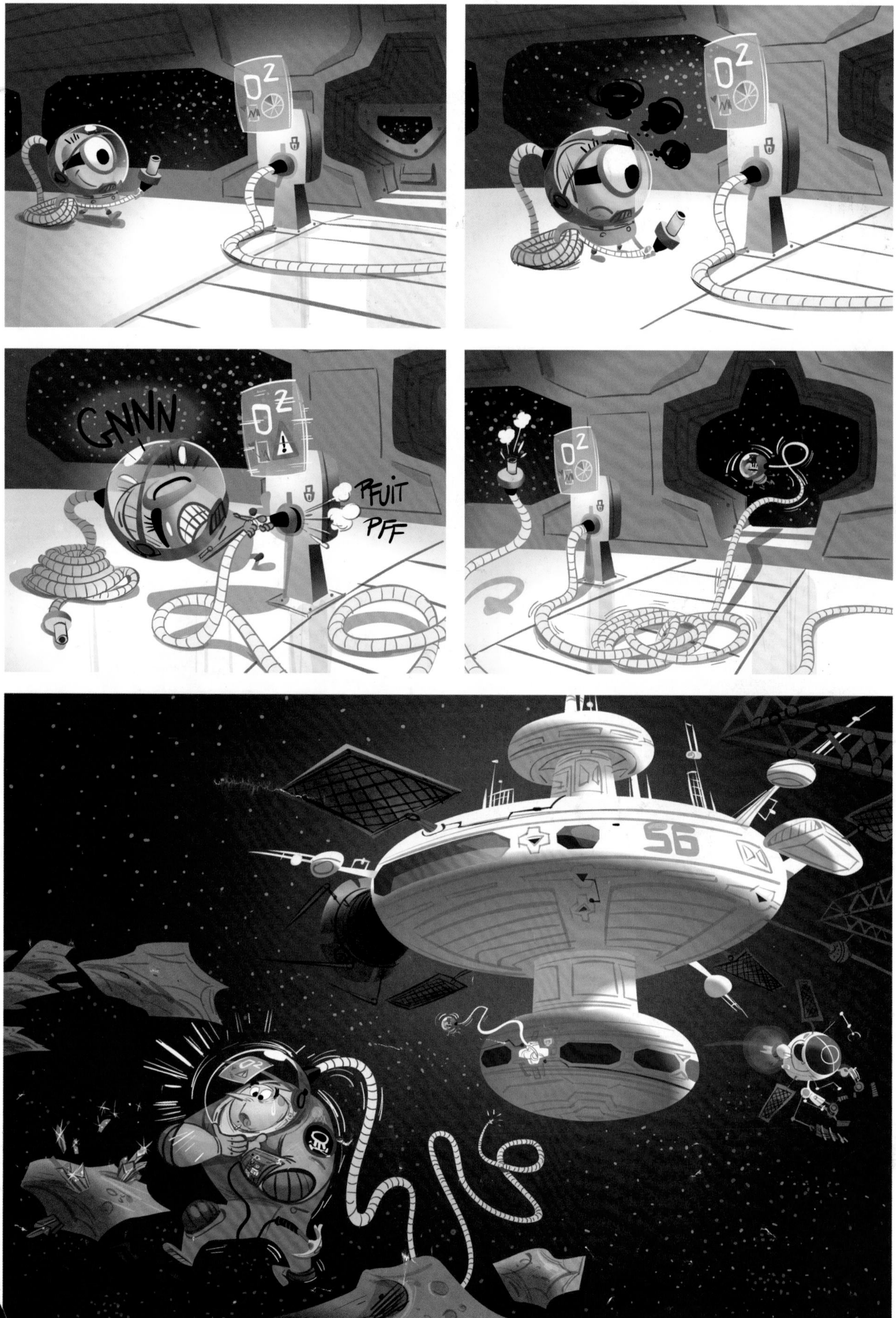
GNNN
PFUIT
PFF
56

Renaud+Lapuss' 2018

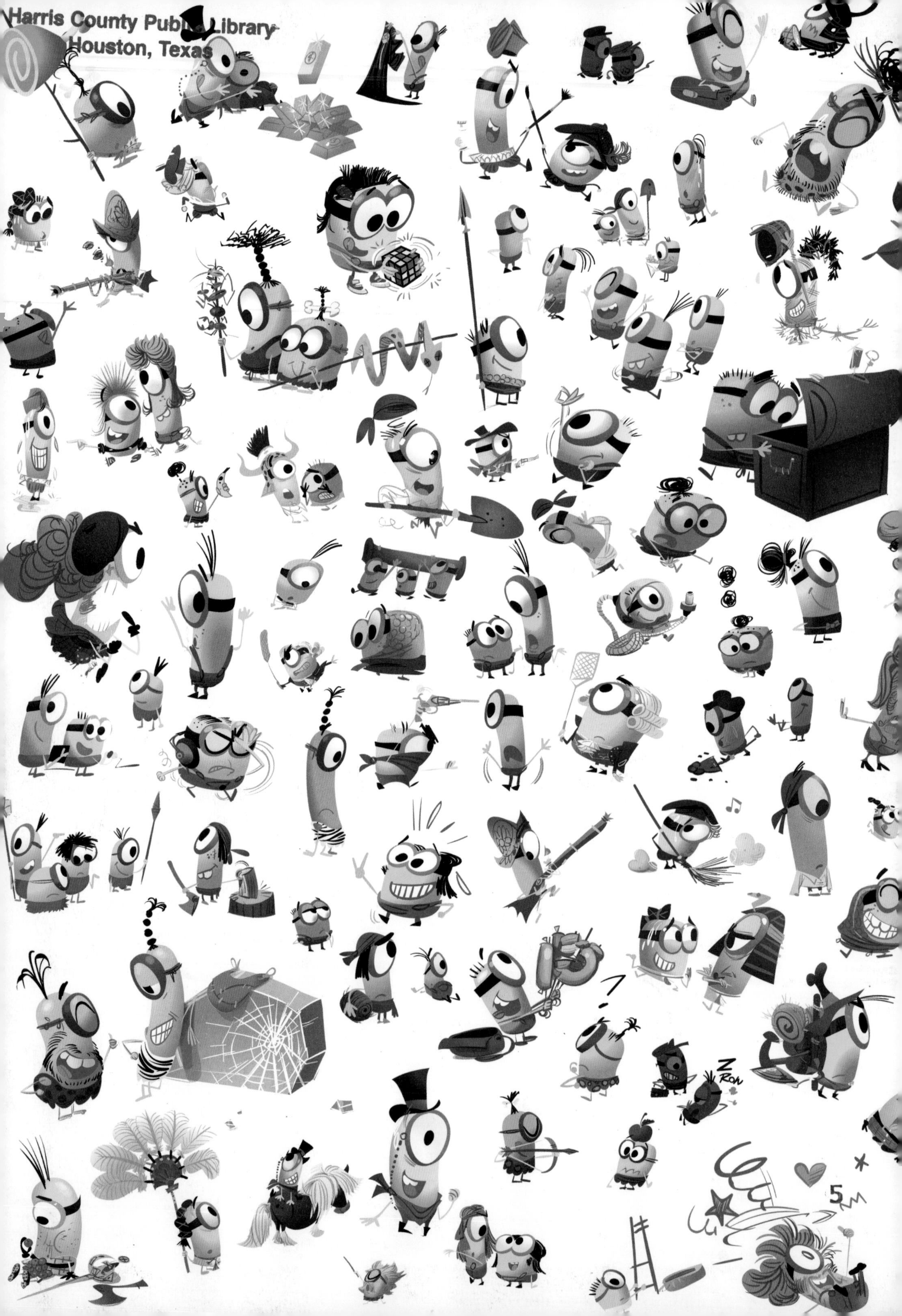